"You can open your eyes now."

She did, but she wanted to close them again when she realized the compromising position she found herself in. The earl cradled her legs with one arm and supported her shoulders with the other. With her arm around his neck, there could be no more than an inch separating their faces.

His glittering blue eyes stared into her own bright green ones, and for some reason Christina found herself a little light-headed. There was something so disturbing about him, so compelling.

What would it be like, she wondered fancifully, *if he kissed me?*

"I should think we ought to be introduced first, don't you?"

With horrified shock, she gasped, realizing she'd spoken her thoughts aloud.

KIMBERLEY COMEAUX is a pastor's wife who wears many hats, including: choir director, women's ministries leader, and Web designer for her church. Her first love, however, remains dreaming up and writing inspirational romances for the wonderful Heartsong readers! She lives in Cajun Louisiana with her husband, Brian; teenage son, Tyler; and their two dogs.

Books by Kimberley Comeaux

Don't miss out on any of our super romances. Write to us at the following address for information on our newest releases and club information.

Heartsong Presents Readers' Service
PO Box 721
Uhrichsville, OH 44683

The Vicar's Daughter

Kimberley Comeaux

Heartsong Presents

To my husband, Brian, for taking me to England and inspiring this story and to my son, Tyler, who shares my love of history

A note from the Author:
I love to hear from my readers! You may correspond with me by writing:

Kimberley Comeaux
Author Relations
PO Box 719
Uhrichsville, OH 44683

ISBN 1-58660-863-0

THE VICAR'S DAUGHTER

All Scripture quotations are taken from the King James Version of the Bible.

All of the characters and events in this book are fictitious. Any resemblance to actual persons, living or dead, or to actual events is purely coincidental.

PRINTED IN THE U.S.A.

one

Christina Wakelin quickly realized the situation had developed into quite a dilemma. When she'd seen the poor old yellow cat, crying while it clung in terror to the unsteady limb near the top of the tree, she'd wanted only to help it down.

So without a care for how unseemly it might be for a young lady to climb a tree or the fact the tree just happened to be on the estate of Lord Nicholas Thornton, the Earl of Kenswick, she set forth to rescue the poor creature.

If only she'd heeded her friend's warning, she would not be in this predicament! Helen, who stood staring up at Christina with worry marring her pretty face, had pleaded several times for her to give up the foolish mission and climb down.

She should have taken the advice earlier, however, because now she could not. Not only was the cat stuck in the tree, Christina feared that she was too. But the fact remained—the cat needed rescuing, and she must try to save it.

"Please, Christina! Do come down," Helen told her in an overloud whisper. "What if Lord Thornton finds you frolicking around in his tree? He hasn't been exactly friendly and sociable since his return. I do not want to even consider what he might do!"

Christina carefully moved her hand to get a better grip

on the branch as she hugged it with both her arms and legs. "Helen, I do not think he could do anything that could be worse than falling out of this tree." She winced as her arm slipped, scraping the tender skin of her wrist. "I don't suppose you could climb up here and help me?"

"I can scarcely go up a flight of stairs without feeling faint from the height, you know that!"

Christina groaned with frustration over her inability to think of a way to get down from her perch and save the cat at the same time.

"Meeeooooow," the scruffy animal cried again as it peered at her with big golden eyes.

"Do not carry on so, Cat. You are the reason I am in this situation in the—ow!. . .first place!" Christina slipped again, this time scraping the palms of both hands.

"Don't tell me you are conversing with that animal," Helen said from below. "What if Lord Thornton should happen to hear you? Why, he'd think you were not only a nuisance but mad as well."

Christina tried again to reach out for the cat, but the contrary animal kept backing away, going farther onto the weaker part of the limb. "Since Lord Thornton has not been seen since his return to Malbury these last four months, I'd say you worry in vain. Besides, Helen, I do not understand this dismal fascination you have for the earl. One would think him a monster by your comments."

"He is a scoundrel, Christina! I dare say there is not one in all of England who has not heard of his exploits. He drinks excessively and frequents gaming halls, and it's been rumored he has participated in two duels. *Two*, Christina!" she emphasized, her voice showing how scandalous she thought it was. "His own fiancée threw him over because she found him in the company of another woman of questionable reputation."

"Perhaps you did not listen to my father's sermon last Sunday when he spoke of how we should not judge our brothers," Christina gently reminded her friend, as she dared to look down at her. Christina was the daughter of the village vicar, a man whose heart-stirring sermons brought parishioners from as far away as Nottinghamshire, ten miles away. "And besides, while I do not know the particulars of his engagement or the duels, I think we can safely assume he has not been gambling or calling someone to pistols since his return!"

Christina tried not to think about how unsteady the branch seemed as she scooted out a little farther. This time she could touch the cat but not quite grab it.

"Christina!" Helen cried out again, this time sounding more alarmed. "Can you not let the cat be and come down? I do believe the branch is bending!"

"Nonsense! I've almost got him," she replied, though she could feel the branch giving way herself.

Just as she had the cat by the scruff of its neck, her attention was caught by someone walking from the house toward them.

"Oh, dear! Helen, it's Lord Thornton and he's headed this way!" she cried in a hushed tone.

Helen's eyes grew round with fright. "Say it isn't so, Christina! What are we to do?"

"You must run, Helen. Leave the grounds before he sees you!"

"But what about you?"

"Surely, he won't see me up here. I'll climb down just as

soon as it is safe."

Helen looked doubtful, but she didn't argue further. Casting a worried last look up to her friend, she started running toward the opening in the fence through which they'd slipped.

Christina turned her eyes back toward the earl. He appeared to be quite a dour, brooding gentleman, not at all like he'd been when he left Malbury years ago. Even his appearance was vastly changed, older and somehow wilder. His black hair was tousled about his face and falling unfashionably past his collar, framing features that were stern and proud with defined cheekbones and a straight, noble nose. He walked with a definite limp that Christina knew must have been a product of the war.

Despite his grim countenance, he was smartly dressed in a dark green riding coat over a tan waistcoat, and his buckskins tucked into polished black Hessian boots encased his long legs. A snow-white cravat about his neck cinched the look and made him appear very much the lord of the estate.

He was nearly at her tree now, and she found herself holding her breath and praying he wouldn't look up. Christina's heart nearly stopped when he paused briefly and looked around, as if he were looking for something.

It seemed to Christina an eternity passed before he finally started to walk away. And just as she thought she might escape his notice, the old tomcat let out a long mournful meow Lord Thornton would have to be deaf not to hear.

Apparently, his hearing was fine, because he immediately turned and looked up into the tree—and directly at her.

His brooding expression turned thunderous. "What. . .?" he growled in unbelief. "You up there, who are you and what are you doing on my estate?"

Christina swallowed and hoped she could somehow talk her way out of this situation without her father finding out. "Uh, I beg your pardon, my lord. I did not mean to trespass, but—"

"I suppose you didn't mean to climb my tree either?"

"Well, no, I didn't actually mean to, but—"

"Yet here you are, trespassing on my land and my privacy," he interrupted, his face stony and unreadable. "Come down at once. Although I should call for the constable, I must find out your identity and return you to your parents."

Christina had many faults, but her worst, as her father frequently reminded her, was her inability to bridle her temper or her tongue. "I would appreciate it if you would refrain from interrupting me and let me explain! Had you looked at my situation up here with a rational mind, you would see I am not alone but am attempting to rescue this poor unfortunate cat!" Unable to lift her hands without falling, she nodded toward the animal that sat looking at her as if it didn't have a care in the world.

"That is *my* unfortunate cat," he said, surprising her.

"Yours?" He did not look like the sort of man who would be a pet owner. "Then what is his name, pray?"

She saw that her question disconcerted him for a moment. "Well, he doesn't have one. I just call him Cat."

"I am not sure that I believe—"

Before Christina could finish her statement, the cat leaped from the limb and sailed down to the next limb, and then the next, until he landed perfectly in the Earl of Kenswick's arms. As she watched the big man cuddle the cat and fondly scratch those scruffy ears, she wished she could leap out of the tree herself and run away. How embarrassing to know her efforts were all for nothing; they served only to put her in an awful standing with Thornton and would probably get her in trouble with her father.

"My patience is wearing thin, Madam. I want you out of the tree this minute," he barked at her, as he let the cat jump from his arms.

Christina bit her lip, trying to decide what to do. She finally decided to confess. "There's just a small problem, my lord."

"And that problem would be?"

"I'm afraid if I move, this branch will break."

He frowned. "Nonsense! The tree is as strong as any you'll find in—"

A loud crack belied his words, and Christina found herself airborne. Frantically she reached out, trying to stop herself, and latched onto a branch full of spring leaves, but not before scratching herself even more in the process. The rough wood cut into the skin of her palms where she held fast to the limb, and Christina knew she could not maintain a grip for much longer.

"Madam! Look down and see where I'm standing. You're not very far up now, so let go and I'll catch you," Thornton called from below in an uncharacteristically gentle tone.

Tears began to well up as Christina forced herself to look down to where the man stood. Not very far? It looked a distance of miles from where she hung. She recalled his limp. "How. . .?" she began, unsure how to ask it. "Your leg, Sir. Won't it hurt?"

"Forget my leg and just let go." When she didn't respond,

he shouted, "I said *now*, Woman!"

The booming command worked better than any gentle coaxing could do. Christina closed her eyes and let go, screaming the whole way down until she hit something solid. Firm, strong arms wrapped around her, and she heard Lord Thornton grunt at the impact. He stumbled a moment and then righted himself.

"You can open your eyes now," he told her with a dry, almost humored, voice.

She did, but she wanted to close them again when she realized the compromising position she found herself in. The earl cradled her legs with one arm and supported her shoulders with the other. With her arm around his neck, there could be no more than an inch separating their faces.

His glittering blue eyes stared into her own bright green ones, and for some reason Christina found herself a little light-headed. There was something so disturbing about him, so compelling.

What would it be like, she wondered fancifully, *if he kissed me?*

"I should think we ought to be introduced first, don't you?"

With horrified shock, she gasped, realizing she'd spoken her thoughts aloud. Like a fly trying to free itself from a web, she scrambled out of his embrace, backed away from him, and began tugging at her dress and smoothing her hair. Hot waves of embarrassment swamped her, and she did what she always did when she got nervous.

She began to prattle.

"Well, that didn't turn out so bad, did it? I mean, the cat's fine, you don't seem too wounded from my crashing into you, and as you can see I've sustained no broken bones, so I'll just run back to my home and leave you to your coveted solitude. I'm sure you're anxious for me to leave, since you all but said so just a minute ago when I was perched in your tree, so I'll say cheerio and—"

"Do be quiet, will you? You've already jarred every bone in my body. Don't add to it by giving me a headache," he snapped, making a show of rubbing his temple.

"Oh, dear! I knew I would wound you! What can I do? Do I need to fetch a servant?"

He put out a hand to stop her from fawning over him, and then he froze. A look of astonishment crossed his features. "I just realized who you are!" he exclaimed, not looking too happy about it. "The red hair, the penchant for getting yourself into messes, the rattling tongue. You're Christina Wakelin, the vicar's daughter!"

Christina was a little insulted that his last statement sounded remarkably like an accusation. "Very good, my lord, now I'll just leave and—"

"It was you who pushed Harriet Cummings into the pond the summer before I left for the war!" he charged, coming toward her with eyes narrowed.

"I thought she could swim," Christina said defensively. "I didn't mean to almost drown her."

"I suppose you didn't mean for me to get blamed for it either?"

Christina swallowed and took another step back. "Well, it was all sort of confusing after she fell in," she explained, knowing the excuse was weak. Actually, Harriet had been teasing Christina cruelly that whole day. Even now Christina didn't understand why Harriet seemed to hate her so much. But Christina, tired of being teased and too immature to think about the consequences, decided on a whim to exact her revenge when she'd seen Harriet walking with Nicholas Thornton along the lake's edge.

"I'm sorry I didn't come forward and take the blame, but that was so long ago, my lord. Surely you can't still be holding it against me. Harriet survived, after all." She tried to smile but erased it once she saw he was not placated by her apology.

"My father almost disowned me over the incident, and my brother was upset I'd ruined his sixteenth birthday party. Not to mention Harriet declared never to speak to me again."

Christina backed up until she hit another tree. "Well, she really wasn't a very good friend, then, was she?" she reasoned with a half-hearted smile.

"I didn't want her for a friend. I intended to begin courting her!"

"Oh, dear."

"That's just one instance. I have a dozen other memories of your mischief!" he emphasized.

"Surely you're not going to list them all," she pleaded, hating that he was correct in his allegations.

"That would take all day."

He looked so peeved, Christina briefly wondered if all the rumors about him were true. Was he such a cad that he would harm a lady?

"But that was so long ago, my lord! Surely you don't hold me accountable for things I did as a child," she reasoned.

He looked at her as if she had just told him the moon were made of cheese. "I don't *if* the person learns her lesson and grows up to be a responsible adult! Did I or did I not just find you in my tree? You, Madam, have not changed."

"You're not going to challenge me to duel are you?" she asked, remembering the conversation she'd just had with her friend.

He shook his head as if he hadn't heard right. "I beg your pardon?"

"Never mind," she answered quickly, wishing she would think before she spoke. "My lord," she began again, "you are wrong in saying I haven't changed. I am a Christian woman and strive to—"

"Don't start handing me any drivel about religion! I lost any faith I might have had years ago."

Christina's heart broke at the bitterness that marred his face and laced his words. "But God can restore—"

"No one can take away the bitterness of war or the contempt I hold myself in for causing my father's death! And now word has come that my brother's ship has been lost at sea. . . ." He seemed to choke on the last sentence and quickly looked away, but not before Christina saw the sorrow that filled his eyes. "Now, if you don't mind, Miss Wakelin, I'll escort you home. But from now on, I'd appreciate you not trespassing or climbing any more of my trees."

Christina wanted to say something to make things better, but she thought it wise to hold her tongue. At least for now. But, being the crusader that she was, she knew she would not let this subject or this man be for long. There had to be a way to help him. Perhaps her father could provide her with answers.

"This isn't London, my lord. My home is only a stone's throw, so I shall see myself home and leave you to your solitude," she told him as she started to go. But when she had taken only a few steps, she turned back to where he stood looking at her. A strange expression filled his eyes as he stared at her, as if he were puzzled by something.

His eyes were the most beautiful shade of blue, and Christina thought she could stare into them for hours. But his sudden frown dispelled any fanciful thoughts she entertained about the earl. A bitter, disillusioned man was not someone to have romantic feelings for. Of course, a mere vicar's daughter had no business entertaining any sort of feelings for a titled man.

"You've changed your mind about needing an escort?" the earl spoke, breaking Christina from her thoughts.

She blinked, embarrassed she'd been staring at him for such a lengthy time. "I only wish to thank you for catching me. I could have come to great harm, had you not been there."

His face was one of cool indifference. "You are fortunate I did not know who you were or I just might have let you hang there."

Christina could not help it; he seemed to be trying so hard to appear the mean-hearted villain that she started to laugh. "Then I thank you for having such a bad memory. Good day, my lord," she told him. Turning from his glowering face, made even angrier by her laughing, she ran to the back gate and off the estate.

two

Nicholas Thornton, the sixth Earl of Kenswick, was not having a good day. He had not had a good day for three days since his encounter with Christina Wakelin. It confounded him, and even irritated him, that he could not seem to get her out of his mind.

He, who had been in the company of the most refined women of England, of whom he had given no more than a passing glance, could not make himself forget the way her eyes sparkled with mischief when she stared down at him from atop the tree.

The past year had been hard on Nicholas. Because of his physical injury during the war, not to mention the mental injury his mind and soul had suffered, he'd been filled with bitterness and self-pity. He wasn't proud of how he spent the last year of his life, living a less than sterling existence—frequenting places no gentleman would enter—but he hadn't been able to stop himself. It was as though he were on a path to self-destruction and couldn't seem to stop.

Which is why he returned to Kenswick Hall, hoping to shut himself away from the world, to find some sort of peace in his solitude. He felt so alone, with his father dead and his brother missing at sea.

Perhaps he was getting his just reward. He felt no hope for himself—no light at the end of his long, dark tunnel.

For exactly four weeks and nineteen days, his mood had grown darker, his attitude so beastly even his servants stayed clear of him.

And then Miss Wakelin climbed his tree, and for the first time in a very long time, he found himself concentrating on someone other than himself.

Perhaps it was because she acted so shockingly. He found himself admiring her daring to have climbed his tree just to save a cat. He had to admit, though, it was rare to see a gentleman's daughter, country-bred or no, so lacking in feminine graces. The vicar had always seemed so capable a person when it came to taking care of the parish. How did that capability not extend to the rearing of his only daughter?

It was a shame really, because Nicholas had to admit she was quite pretty, despite the wild red color of her hair. How would she ever attract a marriage offer behaving as if she were a child?

Not that it was any of his business, Nicholas reminded himself as he stepped onto the balcony overlooking his front lawn. He'd forget about her soon enough and his solitary world would go back to normal.

"My lord," Pierce spoke from the doorway, breaking him from his thoughts. Nicholas turned, noticing that his butler regarded him with the same wary expression most of his staff had adopted around him.

"Yes, Pierce, what is it?" he asked briskly, irritated he was interrupted at all.

"Sir Walter Keen, the solicitor of your brother's estate, is here to see you. I've shown him to the library."

Nicholas replied curtly, "I believe my orders were to turn away anyone who called. You know I don't receive visitors."

He was surprised when Pierce remained in the doorway, nervously clearing his throat. "I beg your pardon, my lord, but I believe that you *must* see him."

Nicholas raised a haughty dark eyebrow. "Must, Pierce?"

"Sir Walter's word, my lord."

He wondered if he hid in the attic, would he be able to get through the day without interruptions? "Then tell him I'll be right down."

Fifteen minutes later, Nicholas opened the door to the library and was surprised to find not only Sir Walter, but also a woman, whose plain dress made him guess she was a servant of some sort. It was the baby she held, however, that made Nicholas uneasy.

Sir Walter, a tall, broad-shouldered man, impeccably dressed, stood up as the earl entered. "I'm so sorry for this inconvenience, Lord Thornton, but a matter of great importance has arisen."

Nicholas glanced over at the woman with the child as she stood and gave him a brief curtsy. He looked back to the solicitor. "It must indeed be an emergency that you had to bring your child along," he commented, before remembering Sir Walter was not a married man.

Sir Walter, apparently, was not one to be intimidated by class or sarcasm. He looked directly into the earl's eyes and told him what Nicholas did not want to hear. "This is not my baby, Thornton. He is your brother's child. Tyler Douglas Thornton he is so named, and now he is yours."

Nicholas looked with horror at the tiny pink infant swaddled in a blanket. "Why cannot Ann, my late brother's wife, care for the child?"

"I regret to inform you that Mrs. Thornton did not make it through childbirth. Of course, you know both her parents are deceased as well as any close relative, and since the baby seems to be your sole heir at the moment, the guardianship for the child falls to you, my lord."

"What about my aunt, Lady Wilhelmina Stanhope? She has a nice home in Stafford, and I'm sure—"

"And she is never there, my lord. She is abroad seven months of the year." He gave the earl a pitying look. "I'm afraid there is no one else."

"Have you utterly lost your senses, Man? You cannot bring an infant and just drop it on my doorstep, expecting me to look after it. I know nothing about raising children!" he exclaimed. How could he be responsible for a helpless, innocent infant?

"I'm sure you can find a competent nanny to take care of the child. I've a list here, in case you need one."

Thornton took the list, crumbled it, and threw it across the room. "This is what I think of your list!" he said, taking a menacing step toward the attorney.

Sir Walter, maintaining his mild expression, sighed. "I hope, for your sake, you'll be able to find that list once I'm gone. You'll need it, I'm sure."

"I think not, since I'm going to make sure that. . .that child goes with you!" He glared at the man accusingly. "There is no possible way I can take care of this child!"

"I find one does what one must when situations arise, my lord." With that, Sir Walter walked past Nicholas to where the butler stood with his hat and coat ready.

Nicholas stared at the back of the retreating man with unbelieving eyes. "You cannot mean to leave, Sir!"

"I do and I must. I have other matters to attend to." He donned his hat and nodded at the woman.

Before Nicholas could bark out another protest, the woman pushed the squirmy bundle into his arms and walked out with Sir Walter.

"Good day, Lord Thornton," the solicitor said with a calmness that made Nicholas seethe.

"Now see here. . . !" His voice drifted to a stop when he realized the solicitor had already left the room.

"I cannot believe this!" he growled under his breath as he started toward the door.

But Pierce, acting out of character, boldly stepped into the doorway, blocking his path. "Shall I see the nursery is made ready for young Master Tyler?"

Nicholas felt a rising panic take over his body. "The only thing I want you to move, Pierce, is your body from my doorway!"

"For what purpose, my lord? The young master is a Thornton. Should not the best place for him be with his closest Thornton relative?"

"You overstep your boundaries, Pierce."

The old butler simply nodded his head calmly. "Yes, my lord."

Nicholas turned away from the butler and went to the window. He watched as Sir Walter's coach pulled away from Kenswick Hall, leaving him with a burden he could not even begin to fathom.

However, he could not deny Pierce's words. The babe was a Thornton and, therefore, since Nicholas had no desire to marry, the future Earl of Kenswick.

If there is a God, he thought, *He surely must be punishing me for all of my misdeeds.*

Almost fearfully, he turned his attention to the child. *What did Sir Walter call him? Tyler Douglas.*

The baby looked at him at that moment and made a cooing sound. He was so tiny, so vulnerable—so innocent. Nicholas may have thought having a baby shoved upon him was highly unfair, but as he looked at those trusting blue eyes, he realized what was most unfair was that the babe should have him for a surrogate father. He, who could not even manage his own life, would now be in control of someone else's.

Even in war he'd not been so terrified.

He looked around and saw that his staff had gathered at the doorway, joining his rebellious butler. They exchanged nervous glances, but they didn't move.

One of the younger maids, whose name eluded Nicholas at the moment, shyly walked into the room. "Pardon me, m'lord, but I believe I know someone who might can 'elp you find a good nanny for the little one there."

Nicholas sighed. "Then by all means find this person and send her to meet me right away." He winced at the desperation he heard in his voice.

How could something so small disrupt his life so thoroughly?

"Right away, m'lord," she said, and, after a quick curtsy, hurried from the room.

Noticing the group of staring servants, Nicholas scowled. "Well, don't just stand there as if there were nothing to do! Someone tell Jennings to ride out to Stafford and fetch my aunt if she is there. And would somebody please take this smelly child. . ." His voice drifted off when he realized no one had stayed to honor his last request.

With a defeated sigh, he turned back to the window thinking his life could not possibly get any worse.

&

For three days, Christina had not been herself. Usually she would go about her business, looking after her sick animals, helping her father with his duties as vicar, as well as researching different topics for her father's sermons. But for three days she could not concentrate on anything. She tried to do needlepoint but kept knotting the thread. She sat to play the piano but hit so many bad notes her father made her stop.

It was all *his* fault. That dreadful man, the Earl of Kenswick.

Oh, she knew their meeting had been all her fault initially, but when she'd been turned away from his door, when she'd called on him, not once, but twice—well, that just infuriated her! To think she'd actually been feeling sorry for him. His butler informed her he wasn't receiving anyone, but she knew he must have given special instructions not to allow her inside the hall. How could he know she wanted to speak to him? She'd wanted only to invite him to church and perhaps help him see that there is a God after all.

Her other reason was to inquire about his cat. Because of talent for mixing herbs, most folks in the area brought their sick pets to her; she wanted to offer her services in case his cat ever needed her.

It was a strange gift, to be sure, but one that was often needed in their small village, whether it a limping workhorse or a sickly hound. The last three days, however, even her animal services had suffered, and she hadn't been able to cure Mrs. Walden's cat from a bout of sick stomach!

Why Thornton's blatant snubbing hurt Christina so much, she had no idea. Maybe it was that she just wanted to make up for her past mistakes. Maybe it was that she wanted to encourage him to attend one of her father's services so he could hear about how God loved him.

Maybe you just find him attractive! She quickly dismissed the thought since, of course, she'd never be attracted to such a rude, boorish man.

No, she was sure her motives were of a noble nature. He was a man made bitter because of war and the death of his father and brother. That was why he'd developed such a terrible reputation—why he fought those duels and broke off with his fiancée.

She would help him. Somehow, some way, she would show him God could truly give him a new life—a brand-new heart.

And that is what Christina prayed. She asked God to open a door of opportunity for her to be able to help Lord Thornton.

A knock sounded at her door, and Mrs. Hopkins, their longtime housekeeper, walked into the parlor where Christina sat. "Miss Cooper to see you, Ma'am."

"Polly! Do come in." Christina welcomed the girl with a smile as she walked into the room. "It's only ten in the morning. Did Mrs. Donaldson give you the day off?"

Polly smiled shyly at Christina as she tucked a wayward strand of hair back into her white ruffled cap. "Oh, no, Ma'am. I don't work for Mrs. Donaldson anymore. I found a post as a 'ousemaid at Kenswick 'all. That's why I've come 'ere."

Christina couldn't have been more surprised. Was this God's answer to her prayer? "Is there something I can help you with?" she queried, trying to appear nonchalant.

"Yes, Ma'am. You see, Lord Thornton is in need of a nanny, and I knew if anyone in the county knew where to find one, it would be you."

Christina could do nothing but stare at the young girl. Finally, she found her voice. "I beg your pardon, did you say nanny?"

The man was a bigger cad than even Helen thought!

"Yes, you see, Lord Thornton's sister-in-law died in childbirth just a few days ago, leaving behind the young master. He was brought to Kenswick 'all a few moments ago, since the earl is 'is nearest relative."

Perhaps she'd been a little hasty in judging the man, Christina thought guiltily. If he were willing to raise the child, then surely he couldn't be all that bad.

"Lord Thornton tried to give him back to the man who brought 'im. You should 'ave seen 'im, Ma'am. I've never seen the man in such a temper, although I've 'eard 'e's rarely in an agreeable mood. But when the earl tried to run after the man, the butler stopped 'im, reminding 'im of 'is duty." She widened her eyes and shook her head slowly. " 'E was none too 'appy about it though, truth be told!"

So maybe he was a little bit of a cad, after all.

"Well," Christina said, standing to her feet. "We must see to this poor infant. I will endeavor to find a nanny, but in the meantime I will see that he is sufficiently taken care of."

Polly eyed her warily. "I'm not sure the earl would like that, Ma'am. 'E doesn't allow anyone 'sides us servants into Kenswick 'all. And sometimes I think 'e'd rather we would just disappear and leave 'im alone!"

Christina marched to the door, pulling the bonnet on her head as she went. "How well I know, Polly. But no matter. I will see to the infant, and Lord Thornton will just have to abide me!"

In an uncharacteristic fit of vanity, she checked her reflection in the hall mirror. She was wearing one of her better morning gowns, with its fashionable high waist and rounded neckline, the light blue color a perfect complement to her complexion. Her hair was a bit messy since, as usual, curly strands had come loose from her topknot, but at least with a bonnet she would look presentable.

As she finished tying the ribbon to her bonnet, Christina cast a quick look upward and smiled. "You not only work in mysterious ways, Lord, You work in a most hasty manner!"

"What's that, Ma'am?" Polly asked.

"Oh, nothing, Polly. I was just thinking aloud," she replied. And as she marched toward Kenswick Hall, she felt somehow empowered, as though she'd been handed a mission only she could fulfill—a crusade to lead a man out of his self-indulgent life and into the light.

three

Christina and Polly entered Kenswick Hall from the servants' entrance and walked through two long hallways before they entered the enormous main hall.

Since she was a little girl, Christina had loved the home with its grand chandeliers and richly dyed carpets. Many times over the years, the former earl and his wife had invited them over for tea or for a small dinner party, and Christina relished the memories of how she'd felt among the tall marble columns and antique tapestries. Huge windows on either side of the door allowed sunlight to pour in and caused the crystal chandeliers to scatter splashes of color throughout the room.

It had truly been a beautiful and happy home.

Now it was a sad and dismal one, because other than the lamps set about the room, every piece of furniture was covered with white dust cloths. "What is all this, Polly? It looks as though the house is not in use!"

"That's the way the master 'as ordered it, Ma'am. 'E says no use in showing off furniture no one's going to see," Polly answered matter-of-factly as she stopped suddenly at a huge double door, causing Christina to bump into her.

"Oh! So sorry."

"It's all right, Ma'am." Polly lifted her hand to knock on the door. "I'll just let 'im know you're 'ere."

"Wait!" she said suddenly as she thought of how she'd

been turned away from the hall in the last few days. "Did you tell him you were bringing me back here to the hall?"

Polly shook her white-capped head. "No, Ma'am. I just said I knew someone who could 'elp 'im."

"Hmm," Christina said. "If that is the case, you'd do well to let me go in first." Polly opened her mouth to disagree, but Christina shook her head. "If you announce it is I you've brought to aid him, then I'm afraid he might not see me."

"But, Ma'am," Polly tried to argue, but Christina ignored her and opened the door herself.

The scene that greeted her was one not even her imagination could have conjured up. There he was—the stern, unsmiling man she'd met earlier, the brooding creature who turned away visitors, the same person who ordered that dust cloths remain on all his furniture—trying to change a diaper.

He was so focused on his task, he did not even hear her enter the room, and she took the opportunity to study him. No longer was his dress impeccable. His dress coat had been thrown over a chair, so he was wearing only his unbuttoned waistcoat, linen shirt, and fawn-colored britches. His cravat was untied and rumpled, and his dark curls looked as if he'd been running his hands through them.

"I do not understand how this simple little cloth could be so difficult to put on you," he muttered to the baby, his fingers fumbling with the thick material. "I daresay someone should devise a simpler way to go about this!"

"Well, if you could accomplish that, I promise every mother in England would rise up, throw King George off his throne, and put you in his place," she announced as she walked in his direction.

The earl's head snapped up at the sound of her voice, and a scowl creased his dark features. "First my tree and now my house. Tell me, Miss Wakelin, do you intrude on everyone's privacy here in Malbury, or do you single me out in particular?"

"Actually, my lord, I'm not intruding, I was invited." She pointed to the desk where the baby lay, waiting for him to finish the job. "I believe if you turn the cloth the other way, you'll find it will fit much better."

He threw her another dark look before focusing on the child. He did as she told him and in no time had the diaper fastened snugly.

He looked a little bemused at what he'd just accomplished. "How could you know such a thing?"

Since Thornton made no effort to pick the infant up despite his squirming, Christina nudged the earl out of the way and lifted the child into her arms. "I am the daughter of a vicar," she answered. "I've stayed in the home of many a young mother who needed time to recover after the baby came."

Christina gently rocked back and forth as she looked into the eyes of the earl's nephew. He looked to be only about a month old, but already his head was full of ink-black curls just like his uncle's. Her heart swelled as she bent to plant a kiss on the soft cheek and breathed in the sweet baby smell. One day, she thought, she would be holding one of her own. She prayed it would be so.

"How is your cat, my lord? I've been wondering how he has fared," she asked, though her eyes were still focused on the baby.

"Never mind about the cat! I have a problem on my hands, if you haven't noticed. And though I'd hoped for someone more experienced in these matters," he paused to look her over with a critical eye. "I suppose you'll have to do."

Although Christina was the grandniece of a baronet, she rarely had the opportunity to be in the company of the upper classes. She had never had a "coming out" and had never attended a ball because her father did not approve. Since her life was so full here in the gentle countryside, she had not been bothered by it. Now, standing before this boorish man, Christina was even more thankful of the vicar's disapproval if this were an example of how society behaved.

Were they all this rude and obnoxious?

Christina smiled stiffly. "I am thrilled you approve."

He apparently missed the sarcasm, since he nodded, then backed away from her and started pacing the room. "The servant girl said you could help me find a nanny, and there is no time to waste. I trust you'll be able to procure someone by nightfall." He stopped in the middle of the room as he finished his sentence and looked at her, lifting an imperial eyebrow for emphasis.

"You must be joking!" she blurted. "Acquiring a nanny is a tedious and sometimes lengthy process, Lord Thornton. Of course, I know a few women whom you could interview for the position, but you must choose one who is right for this household as well as for the child."

Thornton narrowed his eyes. "I am not in the habit of repeating myself, Miss Wakelin, but I'll concede you might not be too bright, so therefore I'll make this one concession." Ignoring her outraged gasp, he continued. "I need someone by tonight. I don't care who it is or how far you have to travel to get her, as long as you have her here by nightfall. Is that clear?"

Christina tried hard to hold her tongue, but it proved to be too difficult. "Perhaps you are right. If I were a bright person, I would have recognized you for the mean-spirited cad you are and not come at all!" She held out the baby to him until he reluctantly took it. "I'll find you a nanny, and not because you are ordering me to do so, but because that poor child needs someone to look after him properly."

She swung around and headed for the door, angry with him for being so arrogant and demanding, and angry with herself for letting his behavior get to her.

"Wait!" he ordered in a tone that stopped her dead in her tracks. It was a voice she imagined he had used on the battlefield.

She turned back. *What now?* she wondered, bracing herself for another tirade.

He spoke only five words.

"Take this baby with you!"

&

One thing Nicholas knew how to do was brood, and he did plenty of it in the hours he waited for the vicar's daughter to return.

His thoughts ran more to the negative than to the positive. *What if she couldn't find anyone?* he thought. Of course, he'd been unreasonable in his request, but he was a desperate man! A man who had no idea how he was going to raise an infant.

He tried to think of someone who might take the child,

but he realized he'd severed most of the relationships with those families who might have helped him.

His behavior and broken engagement had cast him out of society's good graces. And since, the *ton*, as the cream of all English society was referred to, had the ability to make or break someone's reputation, he realized it might cast a shadow on his nephew's future also.

That is, if the poor child survived growing up first.

There was always his aunt Wilhelmina. Perhaps she would agree to take the child on, despite the fact she traveled so much. Widowed at an early age, his aunt had never remarried nor had any children. Perhaps she would like the chance to raise a child.

But his aunt was not in England at the moment, and he had no idea when she would return.

It was ironic that the harder he tried to alienate himself from the world, the more responsibility the world dumped on his lap. He could, of course, live up to his reputation as a scoundrel and dump the child back at Sir Walter's door.

But, surprisingly, he couldn't even contemplate it. Maybe there was some decency left in him after all. A small part that still had honor.

He had no time to dwell on that thought, however, because his library door was pushed open at that moment without so much as a knock, and Miss Wakelin came sailing into the room.

Nicholas was struck dumb for a moment as he took in her flushed cheeks and her wild red hair streaming about her face. Never had he known someone (especially a female, for the ones in his acquaintance had been mild-mannered, dull creatures) who appeared to have such a zest for life. When she'd first gone, he asked his housekeeper about her, and she regaled him with tales of the way Miss Wakelin took care of the animals in town and helped the people in her father's congregation. She was never still, he was told, but always flitting about here and there, finding causes and projects to occupy her time.

She might be a bit odd, but she was also the most fascinating woman he'd ever met.

"Good news, my lord!" she exclaimed as she neared him, clasping her hands together. "I have hired a most suitable nanny, a Mrs. Sanborne, and she comes with high recommendations from the Duke of Northingshire himself!"

Guilt swept over Nicholas as she spoke, for he knew the Duke of Northingshire well. They'd been the best of friends before he went to war. North, as his peers called him, tried to speak to him after his father's death, but Nicholas spurned his offer of friendship.

He could use a good friend now.

But a desperate man couldn't let guilt stand in his way of finding decent help for his situation. Nodding briefly, he gestured toward the sitting area. "Show her in then."

Apparently he did not give her the response she was looking for. "Is that all you can say to me? After the miles I have traveled and the people I have met to make sure your request was carried out?" she asked, clearly put out.

Maybe it was the red hair that caused her to be so passionate about everything. "What more do you want me to say, Miss Wakelin?"

"A simple thank-you wouldn't hurt."

"All right then, thank you. Now show her in, please."

Rolling her eyes, Miss Wakelin whirled around and

strode toward the door. Watching her, Nicholas realized the lady amused him a great deal with her colorful nature. In fact, it was getting harder to maintain a bad mood with her constantly bursting into his life.

How was it possible to hate *and* love the way she made him feel at the same time? It was extremely irritating. *She* was extremely irritating.

When Miss Wakelin brought the older woman into the room, Nicholas first noticed she carried the baby competently in her arms. He noticed, secondly, that she wore the biggest smile he'd ever seen on a human being.

"Lord Thornton! May I say what a stupendous honor it is for me to be in your service! Stupendous!" she gushed as she walked up to him, gently bouncing his nephew in her arms as she went. "Might I add what a stupendous little lad he looks to be. Why, just look at how pleasant a disposition he has! Stupendous, isn't he? Quite stupendous!" She looked up at him with a grin wider than the Thames, as if she expected him to respond to her cheerful greeting.

Frankly, he wasn't sure how to respond to the woman. He'd not been confronted with this much merriment since he was a boy, and he was sure he'd never heard the word *stupendous* used so many times in one day, much less a few seconds.

He looked over at Christina Wakelin. Her green eyes sparkled with mirth as she met his gaze, and he wondered if she had known the woman was such a talker when she'd hired her. Perhaps she knew a woman such as this would get on his nerves, and that was why she chose her.

He would have to keep his wits about him in dealing with Christina Wakelin. She was either extremely crafty or a complete innocent. Either way, she could be dangerous to his peace of mind.

Returning his attention to Mrs. Sanborne, he had to stop himself from flinching at her bright smile. *Just because she's cheerful does not mean she is incompetent,* he told himself.

And besides, in times of desperation, one could not be choosy.

"Yes, well, Mrs. Sanborne, I'm sure Miss Wakelin has filled you in on my situation. I'm glad you could come on such short notice," he told her briskly. "Of course, we need to discuss schedules and salary, but it can wait until the morning." He walked behind his desk and pulled a heavy rope hanging from the ceiling that rang for the servants.

It took only a few moments for his housekeeper to usher the new nanny out. Not before she, however, got in a few more sentences of gratitude and used that dreaded word five more times. He was left alone with Miss Wakelin.

"Well," Christina said in the awkward silence. "I guess since I've solved your little problem, I'll be on my way."

"Not so fast, Miss Wakelin," he countered, taking her arm as she tried to turn toward the door. Surprised, she spun back around and fell forward onto his chest. Nicholas steadied her, but he wasn't prepared for the feelings that coursed through him as he held her.

He looked down at her and their eyes met. Unfortunately, it was embarrassment and not attraction he saw in them as they widened under his inspection. "I daresay I have fallen on you again, my lord," she mumbled as she scrambled from his arms and backed away. With cheeks rising to the color of her hair, she continued, "Was there something else you wanted to say?"

It took a moment for Nicholas to answer, because he was still reasoning in his mind that he could not possibly be attracted to the vicar's daughter. It had been too long since he'd been near a woman, he reasoned. *Yes, of course, that must be it.*

He'd sworn off women months ago. He meant to stand by his decision.

"You will, of course, come by tomorrow," he said in a voice harsher than he'd intended. "I'll leave it up to you to decide whether Mrs. Sanborne is the right nanny for my nephew."

Her embarrassment vanished at his words, but her cheeks were blazing now for a different reason. "I am weary, Lord Thornton, of being ordered about as if I were one of your servants. I have done as you asked, gone above and beyond what any friend would do, considering we are not friends, but it ends right here." She thrust her chin in the air in a show of defiance. "I must insist you handle this situation on your own."

She turned back toward the door, and Nicholas did something he'd done only a few times in his life—he panicked. He could not allow her to leave him stranded (why this was important, he refused to ponder), so he found himself using the only ammunition at his disposal.

Blackmail.

"The church, Miss Wakelin, is it not a part of the Kenswick estate?"

Those words stopped her cold in her tracks. She turned around, gazing at him through wary eyes. "The church is, but our home is not. Our small estate was given to my father by my grandfather, Sir Charles Wakelin."

"I am sure your father enjoys his position as vicar here in

Malbury. It would be a shame if something or someone should do anything to jeopardize it," he said evenly.

Of course he had no plans to make good his threat, and he fully expected her to blow up at him and call his bluff.

She did neither. Instead, she studied him calmly, as if trying to see past his haughty façade and read his true thoughts.

When she finally did speak, her words cut him straight to the bone. "Lord Thornton, you had only to ask for my help instead of yelling orders at me, and I would have been glad to comply. Truly, the events that have led to your withdrawal from society and your abandonment of all gentlemanly behavior must have been great, indeed, for you to treat a lady so abominably.

"I am also sorry you have no shame in using blackmail to get your way. But you must understand that God is greater than your threats and even greater than the building you are using for ammunition. That is all it is— just a building. God's church is everyone who believes on Him. If you take away our walls, we will not cease to exist but will simply find another place to join together and worship Him."

Miss Wakelin was wrong. Nicholas was feeling his shame most acutely. "Miss Wakelin, I—"

"Say no more, my lord. I shouldn't have gotten angry at your suggestion, and I apologize. I've suddenly remembered why I came here today. I felt God had opened a door for me to help you. You see, I'd been praying He would ever since I fell out of your tree," she said with a sad smile. "God has, evidently, not closed the door, so you can count on me to assist you in any way I can. And, of course, I want to do all I can for young Tyler. I'll call directly after breakfast tomorrow."

So stunned was he that *she'd* apologized to *him*, he could not get out a reply before she quit the room.

four

The morning came too quickly for Christina, who had not slept well at all during the night. What was it about the autocratic man that disturbed her so? He was much like all the other nobles she'd ever been acquainted with—self-absorbed, haughty, and so unaware of the lesser classes beneath them.

Not wanting to dwell on him more than she should, Christina chose a pale yellow day dress, accented with blue ribbon around its high waist and cap sleeves. The spring color brought a little cheer to her mood, and she determined by the time she walked downstairs to the breakfast table that she'd be her normal sunny self.

And she was, especially when she saw her friend Helen sitting at the table with her father.

"Helen!" Christina exclaimed as she took her seat to the left of her father and across from her friend. "What brings you to us so early?"

"Why, it's all over the village, Christina, so I had to come hear the news from your lips straightaway!" The fact that Helen said this as if she were shocked made Christina wary.

"Um, I'm not sure what you heard. . . ."

"I'd like to hear your explanation as well, Daughter. I heard from Cook you arrived home at a late hour last night," Reverend Wakelin interjected. "What kind of mischief are you about now that concerns that scalawag, Thornton?"

Christina swallowed as she looked from Helen to her

father. "I have only been assisting his lordship in procuring a nanny for his young nephew. Yesterday I traveled all over the shire until I found one suitable."

Helen's eyes glinted. "That's not what I heard from my maid, who got the news directly from one of Lord Thornton's kitchen help! She said. . ." Helen paused for effect and leaned forward, causing the ribbons of her dress to dip into her orange marmalade. "She said you visited Lord Thornton's home not once but twice yesterday!"

"Yes, but there was a perfectly good reason—"

"Lord Thornton is not a gentleman I would see you associate with, Christina," her father interjected. "From all accounts I would say he is considered the scoundrel of all English society."

Helen sniffed. "I tried to tell her the very same thing, Reverend Wakelin, but she quoted one of your sermons to me and demanded I not judge him."

A grin formed on the vicar's face, though Christina could tell he tried to hide it. "Ah, so you do listen to some of the things I preach about."

"Of course, I do, Father, and I heed every word."

"If that is true, then it must have been someone else who trespassed on Lord Thornton's property and climbed his tree," he responded dryly.

Christina threw a disgruntled look at Helen, but she quickly threw up her hands in defense. "I never said a word!"

"Of course not," the vicar seconded. "I heard it from Cook, just this morning."

Christina took a careful sip of her hot tea. "I think the servants gossip entirely too much. Something should be done about it."

Her father only gave her an indulgent smile. "You only think so, Daughter, when the gossip concerns you."

Christina sighed as she buttered her bread. "You have a point, Father—one that may not be entirely accurate, but a point all the same." She looked up to find her father giving her one of those I-can-see-right-through-you stares, so she felt the need to blurt, "Oh, all right. I suppose I should confess my true reasons for helping the Earl of Kenswick."

Helen slapped her hand on the table. "I knew it!" she declared with a triumphant smile. "I knew you were in love with the earl! I did not believe the excuse about the cat for a minute!"

Christina prudently didn't remind Helen it was she who'd sent Christina after it in the first place. "Helen, I do believe that is the silliest thing I've ever heard come from your lips. I'd sooner fall in love with that ragged cat of his than waste my feelings on him." She took another sip of tea and patted her mouth daintily with her napkin. "You can be assured Lord Thornton feels exactly the same way about me. He was quite put out when he realized who I was that day at the tree."

Helen leaned back in her chair and smiled dreamily. "How romantic! He remembers you from childhood."

"You misunderstand me."

"I would imagine his lordship remembers how Christina used to follow him and his brother all around the village," Reverend Wakelin inserted dryly.

Christina put out a hand. "Please go no further. Lord Thornton has already listed my numerous misadventures, and I'd rather not hear them again, thank you!"

"So, if it's not to secure Lord Thornton for a husband, just what are your plans concerning him?" Helen asked.

Christina took a breath as she looked from her father to Helen. "I fear it concerns his spiritual condition," she began and told them about his life since he'd come home from war, how embittered and hopeless he seemed. "And the worst thing is he no longer has faith in God. From what I can understand, he feels God has abandoned him and his family. I feel it's my duty to help him see God loves him."

The teasing light from her father's eyes was soon replaced with concern. "Christina, I know you think you can help him, and that's extremely commendable of you, but I fear you'll be taking on more than you can handle. I wasn't joking when I said Thornton has garnered quite a bad reputation in London. Any sort of connection with him might not be prudent, no matter how noble the reason."

"But I've already given my word, Father. He's expecting me this morning."

Christina gazed imploringly at her father, a look that served her well when it came to winning an argument.

With a heavy sigh, Reverend Wakelin stood from the table and stared down at both young women. "If you must go, then I insist Helen go with you," he said in no uncertain terms.

Helen, whose one goal in life was to marry a titled gentleman, was not going to pass an opportunity to rub shoulders with one when presented, no matter how much of a scoundrel she believed Lord Thornton to be. "Of course I'll go with her."

Stifling the moan Christina felt rising within her, she gave into her father's demand. "Yes, that will be fine. I should have thought of it myself," she told them, all the while wondering how she was going to explain the presence of yet another person barging into Lord Thornton's self-imposed solitude.

❧

Because Nicholas had trouble falling asleep the night before, it seemed only minutes had passed when he heard the discreet cough beside his bed. Which was odd, really, considering he'd ordered his bedroom strictly off limits as long as he occupied it. That especially meant the morning, so if he chose to sleep until noon, there'd be no one to bother him in his slumber.

He tried to turn away from the sound, but to no avail. Another cough rang throughout his bedchamber—this time a bit louder and more than a bit closer.

"Go away," he commanded without moving or opening his eyes.

"I fear I cannot, my lord," came the starchy reply.

Nicholas realized this was a voice he did not recognize. Like a shot, he turned and sat up, glaring at the tall skinny stranger with narrowed, wary eyes. "Who are you?" he demanded.

Undaunted, the young man straightened his stiff posture even more and thrust his pointed chin in the air. "The name is Smith, my lord, your new valet."

Nicholas wondered if perhaps he was still asleep and only dreaming he'd been awakened. Even better, maybe he'd dreamed all of yesterday—the baby, the nanny, and that annoying Miss Wakelin too.

"Are you all right, my lord?"

He sighed, knowing that even in his sleep he could not dream up such a grating voice.

"I do not have a valet," Nicholas growled, ignoring the young man's question.

"You do, today, my lord. Pierce, a cousin of mine on my mother's side, hired me just this morning. I was told to start right away."

"Well, it all makes perfect sense now," Nicholas grumbled as he got out of bed and walked over to his washbasin. "Only one related to Pierce could annoy me as much as he does."

He grabbed a linen cloth from the dresser and wiped the moisture from his face. "You can go back downstairs and inform your cousin I have no need of your services, and if he keeps overstepping his bounds, I won't have need of his either!"

The young man shook his head. "My lord, it is my opinion that all gentlemen need a valet's services."

"This one does not, so take your opinions and leave, Man!" he shouted.

"In order to properly bring up one's heir, a gentleman needs to bring order to his life so he can be a proper example. That is why my services are needed, my lord," Smith stated as if he were quoting.

"Did Pierce tell you that?"

"My father did, my lord. He is the valet to the Duke of Northingshire."

"Wait a minute," Nicholas interjected. This was the second time in two days North's name had been mentioned. "Is he orchestrating this whole affair? Because if he is. . ."

"I beg your pardon, my lord?" Smith queried, his puzzlement authentic.

Nicholas stalked to the door that led to his dressing chamber. "Never mind, just leave. I'll deal with you *and* your annoying cousin after breakfast."

He slammed the thick oak door behind him, but he could hear Smith from the other side. "Very good, my lord. And I hope the blue coat I laid out for you meets with your approval. I thought it the most appropriate for meeting your nephew this morning."

Nicholas stared at the carefully laid out blue coat and black trousers. Just for spite, he knocked them aside and pulled a green one from his collection.

&

A housemaid escorted Christina and Helen to the nursery on the second floor of the west wing upon their arrival. There they found Mrs. Sanborne rocking the baby.

Already, Christina could see the staff had been hard at work bringing life into the old room with fresh linens, newly polished furniture, and warm rugs in pastel shades on the wood floors.

"Ah, stupendous! My dear Miss Wakelin, I was hoping you'd pay us a visit," Mrs. Sanborne sang out in her enthusiastic way. Her bright eyes turned to Helen. "And you've brought a friend! Why, that's stupendous!"

"This is Miss Helen Nichols. Helen, Mrs. Sanborne is young Tyler's new nanny." The two women nodded to one another, but Christina's eyes were all for the baby.

"Oh, do let me hold him, Mrs. Sanborne. I've thought of nothing else since I left here yesterday," she confessed as the nanny gently handed Tyler into her arms.

Mrs. Sanborne grinned proudly. "My, you look quite stupendous holding that child. I must say you should marry and have some of your own."

Helen took one of the baby's tiny hands into her own. "It has been difficult during the war for any of us country misses to procure a husband with all our men off fighting," she replied, her voice sad.

"'Tis true," Mrs. Sanborne agreed. "But isn't it lucky his lordship was able to come home and be here for his dear nephew?"

"I don't think 'his lordship' appreciates his good fortune, though. I think it shall be up to us to help him realize it," Christina declared as she bent to kiss the baby's soft cheek.

"I did not appreciate the silence of this old house until it was bombarded with the silly chatter of women and a crying baby," Thornton said from the doorway, his voice filled with disdain. He scanned the room until his eyes landed on Helen. "And who are you? It seems my house is overrun by strangers this morning."

Christina turned to him at the sound of his voice, and for a moment she felt her pulse quicken. And because she did not want to feel excitement where this rogue was concerned, she retaliated with sarcasm. She managed to execute an overly dramatic curtsy while holding the baby with one arm and fanning her skirt with the other. "My Lord Thornton, we are so glad you have graced us with your estimable presence this morning, and, yes, we are all quite well. Thank you for inquiring."

Their eyes clashed and held—Christina's matching the challenge in the earl's stare.

The silence in the room grew thick. "My lord!" Mrs. Sanborne burst out. "How good of you to come see after your dear nephew. What a stupendous sleeper he is too."

Seeing how Mrs. Sanborne's favorite word was affecting the earl, Christina felt laughter bubbling up within her. Though she tried to stifle it, she found she could not.

It was the proverbial straw on the camel's back. "Mrs. Sanborne, could you please cease in your use of that irritating word!" he barked out. "And have you no sense, Miss Wakelin, not to laugh in the face of a lion!"

Mrs. Sanborne abruptly stopped her chatter, and both she and Helen took several steps away from him. Truthfully, Christina wanted to run, but she'd sooner be stung by a hundred bees than let the earl see her fear.

"Woke up on the wrong side of the bed, did we?" Christina observed lightly. "Perhaps a little breakfast will set your mood aright. We wouldn't want to scare a poor helpless baby with our voices, now would we?"

They both looked down at Tyler, and to Christina's chagrin, he was looking at his frowning uncle with bright eyes, blowing bubbles from his tiny mouth.

The moment he saw her staring at him, however, his face returned to its usual expression. "I'd say he's none the worse for wear," he muttered. Then, as if he were suddenly in a hurry to escape, he nodded stiffly and left the room.

five

Soon after their encounter, the Earl of Kenswick sent his butler to inform the women that under no circumstances was he to be disturbed. Mrs. Sanborne would direct all problems to the new valet or send for Christina. He did not want reports on how his nephew was faring, nor did he want to visit him. He just wanted to be left alone.

Christina, of course, thought this was ludicrous and had no qualms about disobeying his order, but doing so was much harder than she anticipated.

In fact, nearly a fortnight had passed and not once had she gained an audience with the earl.

How was her plan ever going to work if she could not talk to him or get him to see his nephew? Doubts began to plague her. Maybe the earl really was a lost cause. Maybe not even she could reach him.

Every day she prayed God would give her guidance, and every time she prayed, she felt God did not want her to give up on him.

So she decided to persevere—and become a little devious. Several times she was able to catch him coming from the library or walking in the garden when he thought she had already left the estate. Still, he would either ignore her or tell her he had no desire to converse.

Christina became so dispirited at her thwarted attempts to help him that she stopped seeking him out. In fact, she came to the decision by week's end that she'd no longer go to Kenswick Hall except for the occasional visit to Mrs. Sanborne and the baby. The nanny was doing an excellent job, and it was silly to keep coming when there was no need.

On the particular morning she made her decision, Pierce appeared in the garden telling Christina that Lord Thornton wanted to speak with her in his study.

Curious and elated, Christina nodded to the butler and began to follow him when Helen grabbed her by the arm. "Christina, you cannot think to meet with the earl alone. I must go with you!"

Christina knew she would not be able to speak to Lord Thornton frankly if Helen was in the room. Besides, she'd waited so long to speak with him that she didn't want to share the moment with Helen. Of course, he would be upset to see Helen there too, making him change his mind about seeing her altogether.

Quickly she thought of an alternative. "Pierce," she said. "Is there a window in the study that overlooks the garden?"

Pierce frowned. "Yes, Miss Wakelin, 'tis over there directly in front of us."

"There, you see, Helen? You can stay outside with the baby and watch us from the window. I can assure you, all will be very proper."

"Oh, I see," Helen said slowly. "You want to speak to Lord Thornton *alone*."

"I don't believe you 'see' at all, Helen, and I know I don't like what you're trying to imply," Christina replied.

"If you say so," Helen said with a casual shrug.

Knowing she was not going to convince Helen there was

nothing between the earl and herself, Christina sighed with frustration and headed toward the house.

Pierce led her to the study, where she found Lord Thornton studiously looking over what appeared to be a ledger. He glanced her way and mumbled something about being with her in a moment, then returned his attention to his desk.

Christina squelched the hurt feelings that were once again aroused inside her. Forcing herself not to dwell on his snobbery, she realized it was the perfect time to open the heavy velvet curtains that covered the window. Not only would it allow Helen to see in, it would brighten the otherwise dark and depressing room. With purpose, she pushed the curtains aside, allowing the brilliant sunlight to fill the room.

The earl's response was immediate. "If I'd wanted the curtains open, I would have opened them. Close them. Now!"

Instead of obeying his command, Christina turned to look squarely at him. "Why?"

He blinked, clearly not expecting his wishes questioned. "I beg your pardon?"

"Why do you want them closed?"

"Because I don't like them opened."

Christina felt a shiver of apprehension run up her spine at his deceptively soft tone. Swallowing, she made herself stand firm. "From what I can tell, there is not much you do like."

For a moment, she thought she saw a slight smile curve his lips, but it was so brief, she supposed she must have imagined it. "You're right. There's not much I do like anymore. Now, close the curtain."

At those words, Christina put a hand to her chest and stepped toward him. "But that is so sad! How can you live like that?"

"I was living it very well until you came crashing into my life, disrupting my peace at every opportunity."

He sounded so much like a disgruntled little boy that Christina laughed. "I might have crashed into you once, but I'm not the one who dropped a baby on your doorstep." She folded her arms and gave him a direct look. "And let's not forget, I might have stayed out of your life had you not brought me back into it."

He stood and walked around his desk toward her. Christina felt momentarily breathless at how handsome he looked stepping into the sunlight. "Ah, but you accepted the invitation, as I recall, to have a go at making me see the error of my ways, or something like that, did you not?"

Christina prayed her admiration for him did not show in her face as she stared up at him. Focusing on his question, she replied bluntly, "It's hard to help someone who will not even talk to me." She looked away deliberately with a small shrug. "One might think you were a little afraid of being in my presence."

"All men are wary of women when they're on a mission to reform them," he said as he stepped around her and walked toward the window.

She turned to see that he was about to close the curtains. "No!" she cried as she ran after him, putting a hand on his arm to stop his movement. "I have the curtains open because I cannot be in here with you without some sort of chaperone. If you had good manners, you'd realize that very fact!"

He stopped but did not move his arm from her grasp. A puzzled expression filled his eyes. "Are you not alone with me right at this moment?"

"Not with Helen watching us from the window." She waved at her friend in the garden.

Thornton's eyes narrowed in contemplation. "Watching a couple through a glass pane does not exactly constitute a chaperone."

"I know that, but Helen is just a simple country miss and does not know all the rules of society. I fear I have taken advantage of her on that score," she admitted, feeling slightly ashamed of herself.

"Where as you are a sophisticated lady of society, hmm?"

If he thought to embarrass her, he was mistaken. "Of course I'm not. I've simply had the advantage of being tutored by an aunt who believes all young ladies should have knowledge of society's rules, whether they need it or not." She peered out the window at the two women playing with the baby.

Thornton gave a loud sigh and walked away from her. "Well, now that your reputation is safe, will you please have a seat so I can discuss something with you?"

Christina hid a smile at his disgruntled tone and sat where he indicated.

Lord Nicholas Thornton leaned back in his large cushioned chair and stared broodingly at her for a moment. "Whether you think I'm afraid of speaking to you or not, Miss Wakelin, I'd appreciate it if you'd cease in your efforts to track me down. It has become a little irritating to find you skulking about every corner that I—"

"Oh, I wouldn't call it skulking."

"In those lessons your aunt so generously taught you, I don't suppose there was a lesson on proper etiquette when conversing, was there?" he barked out, clearly irritated she'd interrupted him.

"Yes, I do believe there was," Christina said pleasantly, while picking up a small figurine from his desk. "I must not have felt up to listening that day, though. But, please, do continue."

He began to speak, but Christina's attention was fixated on the expertly carved tiger that was no more than three inches long. Great care had gone into creating each feature, from the expressive eyes to the menacing claws on all four paws.

"This is incredible!" she cried out. "Do you know the person who carved this?"

"I did," he said with a frown. "Now, can we get back to what I was—"

"You did? Unbelievable!"

"Why does that seem so unbelievable?"

"Oh, I didn't mean it that way," Christina said, realizing she must have hurt his feelings. "I just meant I never knew you had such a wonderful talent."

He dismissed her compliment with a wave of his hand. "It's nothing but a hobby. I've just had more time to indulge in my craft lately, which brings me back to what I was saying. My privacy is—"

"So you haven't just been brooding and feeling sorry for yourself. You've actually been expressing your feelings through art!" She held up the tiger to inspect it again. If he could create beautiful figurines like this, somewhere deep inside was a man who was worth saving—a man who saw beauty in life despite his bitterness and grief.

Her statement seemed to bother him. "I do not 'express' myself, as you call it. I was merely indulging in a hobby."

She tried to hide her disbelief. "Of course you were, my lord."

"What? No argument?"

"Why argue, when I know that *you* know I'm right."

He leaned forward, his hands palm-down on the desk. "This is exactly why I need to speak with you. You seem to be on a quest to disrupt my life at every turn, and I would like to know why you feel so compelled to help me, as you call it."

She smiled at him, silently thanking God for the door He'd just opened before her. "The answer is simple, my lord. I'm trying to make you realize you are special to God and to your nephew. Too special to allow yourself to be locked away from the world."

❧

Nicholas sat stunned at her words. Not just because she had the audacity to speak to him so freely, but because her words touched something deep within his heart.

He'd told himself time and time again he didn't need anyone. He'd done and seen horrific things during the war, and he had allowed his self-pity, upon his return to England, to destroy his father's health. He'd been engaged to a nice young woman who didn't deserve the disservice he paid her by breaking their engagement. And he mourned a brother he should have spent more time with.

He'd convinced himself he deserved to be alone. Little did he realize the loneliness would consume him to the point of madness. In the past, he'd enjoyed the company of others—always surrounded by friends and fellow officers.

To be constantly alone was not an easy state to maintain, no matter how much Nicholas thought he deserved it.

Especially with such a lovely, vivacious young woman within his household.

How often had he watched her from the window of his library as she played with his nephew or laughed with her friend? Christina Wakelin made him wish for things he had no right to wish—that he'd been a better man, maybe even a whole different person.

It was ironic that he, a man who once put such a high regard on his status and title, was attracted to a mere vicar's daughter.

He'd acknowledged that truth three days ago when she'd caught him down in the garden. She came walking up to him, holding his nephew, and cheerfully dumped the child in his arms.

Nicholas almost dropped him he'd been so surprised. Fortunately, he recovered fast enough to just as quickly transfer him back to Christina.

Couldn't she understand he was actually afraid he'd fail Tyler just as he had all the others in his life?

"I don't want anyone's help, Miss Wakelin. Now, if you'll excuse me, I—"

But Christina interrupted him. Maybe he'd hoped she would. "But Ty needs your help, Lord Thornton. He's beginning to respond to our faces, and I think it would provide more of a balance in his life to see a man's face as well as a woman's." She stepped closer to the desk. "Every boy needs a father in his life, and you are the closest he will ever have."

The brunt of her words hit him squarely in the conscience. "I'll give you this much, Miss Wakelin, you certainly know what strings to pull to get what you want."

For the first time since she walked into his room, he saw her cheery smile turn into a frown. "You make me sound calculating, and I'm not that way at all!"

"I believe I would use the word cunning." He studied her thoughtfully. "Don't think I haven't noticed how you manage to make everyone around here do exactly what you want. Most of the time, you make them think it was their idea instead of yours."

"I simply treat people the way I would like to be treated, with kindness and concern. That is why they—" she suddenly stopped. "Wait one minute! Have you been spying on me?"

"I was observing, nothing more," he answered with a shrug. "I had to make sure you and Mrs. Sanborne were giving sufficient care to my only heir."

She stared at him and then seemed to accept his answer. "Since you seem to care a little for your nephew's welfare, can you agree to at least spend time with him once a day?"

"Only if you are there too. I refuse to spend too much time in that Sanborne woman's presence."

Christina laughed. "I promise she's not as annoying as you think."

Nicholas shuddered. "I don't care. Either you are there or there's no visit."

"Of course I will be there, but," Christina paused, then continued cautiously, "I don't understand why you've just chastised me for forcing my presence on you, and now you are blackmailing me to be with you every day. I'm afraid I'm a little at sea, Sir."

Nicholas felt like the idiot she just described. What was the matter with him? What had possessed him to make such a stipulation?

Because you are attracted to her, a little voice whispered in his mind. *Because she makes you feel more alive than you've felt in years.*

Something deep inside him wanted to reach out and take the friendship she was offering, but another feeling warred within him at the same time. Guilt and fear would not allow him to act on his attraction, but neither would they stop him from spending a little time in her sunny presence.

"You simply presented a good argument and I have reconsidered. I've seen how good you are with the babe, and I thought he would be more comfortable with you in the room," he said by way of excuse.

Those green eyes of hers seemed to see too much as she studied him warily. He was terrified she could read his thoughts. But then she smiled at him and stood up from her chair. "That's a nice way of putting it."

He stood also. "Shall we meet after the noon hour?"

She was clearly surprised he wanted to meet so soon, but she agreed. "That will be fine, my lord. Until then," she answered with a small bow and left the room.

six

"I don't know what to do with 'em, Miss. My papa says 'e'll be throwing 'em into the river 'n be done wi' 'em if I don't find 'em a 'ome," little William Potts told Christina. Tears made dirty streaks down his freckled cheeks. Six newborn puppies squirmed about in the weathered wooden crate he was holding.

Christina looked worriedly at Helen and then back at the puppies. She'd been summoned to her own home by their housekeeper just as she was about to go with Mrs. Sanborne to meet the earl. "William, these pups look too young to be given away. Where is the mother dog?"

"Got run over by a coach, she did."

"Oh, dear!" Christina cried, her heart always soft toward animals. *And to little boys*, she silently added as she looked at the six year old. "I suppose you want me to care for them?" she asked, although she already knew the answer. It wasn't the first time she'd had to nurse puppies whose mother had died or rejected them. Normally she had plenty of time for such things, but now she had so much on her mind.

As the boy nodded, Christina sighed. "I suppose I'll have to take them then." She took the crate from him and sent him on his way.

"Your father warned you there was no more room for animals, Christina!" Helen reminded her. "He's not going to be happy you've taken on more."

57

"I was just thinking the same thing," Christina admitted, smiling down at the defenseless little creatures. "I suppose I'll just have to find somewhere to put them at Kenswick," she said as a plan formulated in her mind.

"Oh, no, you cannot risk it. If Lord Thornton finds out about them, he'll be furious."

"You're probably right."

"There's no probably to it! You know he will be!"

Christina threw Helen a confident look as she shifted the crate for a better hold. "Then we will just make sure he doesn't find out!"

Helen shook her head and groaned. "You have more temerity than brains! This will be worse than the tree incident, I just know it."

"I've come to realize the earl is not as bad as we first thought. He growls and frowns a lot, but he's mostly harmless." She turned and began walking back to her house so she could get some needed supplies. Helen followed her.

"Mostly harmless?" Helen shrieked. "Do you call participating in two duels mostly harmless?"

"Really, Helen, you bring that up so often, I think you must be a little fascinated by it."

"Nothing about that man fascinates me!" Helen stated firmly.

Christina thought Helen protested too much, but she decided not to pursue it. If anyone had a problem with being fascinated by the earl, it was she.

❧

". . .and it is stupe. . .I mean magnificent how Master Ty is learning to roll, and just yesterday he. . ." Mrs. Sanborne prattled on, but the earl had only one thing on his mind at the moment.

Christina had not come.

Hurt and angry, he barely heard what the nanny was saying to him. For ten minutes she'd talked nonstop, enumerating the tiniest details of what the child had been doing. He tried unsuccessfully, several times, to break into the conversation to ask where Christina was.

Finally he could take no more. "Where is she?" he interrupted in a booming voice.

Mrs. Sanborne swallowed hard before she spoke. "I beg your pardon, my lord?"

He made a sweeping motion toward the door with his hand. "Christina. Why isn't she here with you?"

Mrs. Sanborne's face cleared as she smiled. "Oh! Why, she was called back to her home just before our meeting. I apologize, but she asked me to let you know, and I forgot."

The anger immediately faded, and in its place came a relief so fierce it astounded him. Pointedly ignoring that last feeling, he inquired, "I trust everything is all right with her? Her father is not ill?" He was more concerned than he wanted to be.

"I do not think so, but I cannot be sure," she answered with an apologetic smile.

Preoccupied, Nicholas walked over to the window and peered outside. "Did she say when she would return?"

"No, my lord." Nicholas heard a rustling sound and knew the woman had walked up behind him. "Would you not like to hold the baby for a moment, my lord?"

Nicholas turned, his eyes fastening on the baby, who already bore a remarkable resemblance to him and his brother. He nodded curtly to the nanny and stood still as she placed the baby into his arms. Nicholas had never felt more awkward and inadequate in his entire life. What did one *do* when holding an infant?

The baby must have sensed Nicholas's unease because he squirmed and cried.

Dismayed, Nicholas quickly gave him back to the nanny. "Here, take him," he ordered, but to his utter amazement, and irritation, she just shook her head and laughed.

"Oh, he's just not used to you yet. Bounce him a bit and he'll be just fine," she assured him.

Nicholas scowled at the woman, only to be met with that same amused expression. First his butler, then his unwanted valet, and now the nanny. Did no one take his orders seriously anymore?

"Bounce him," she urged again, when he remained stock-still. "You might even try humming a tune. Babies like that, you know."

"I do not hum," he muttered, but as silly as it felt, he did begin to bounce the baby.

He didn't know what bouncing was supposed to accomplish, and apparently the baby didn't either, because he only cried harder.

Suddenly, like a miracle, the baby stopped crying. Incredulously, Nicholas stared down at the infant and noticed something had caught Ty's eye. Following the direction of his gaze, he turned and saw Christina standing in the doorway.

Uncle and nephew together took in the sight of the vicar's daughter with her curly red hair, held back by a yellow ribbon. Her face was aglow from the outside air, and the sparkle in her green eyes seemed to be solely for him.

He quickly looked away, dismissing the direction his thoughts had taken, but he just as quickly looked back. This time, his eyes fastened on her yellow dress.

"Your dress has dirt on it," he observed with a disapproving frown.

Christina glanced down and shrugged. "Only a little. I'm sure Mrs. Hopkins can get it clean with no problem."

Nicholas had never known a female who wouldn't immediately change for even one tiny speck of dirt. Ladies, he observed, were generally vain creatures. They were educated mostly in music and art and had extensive knowledge of needlepoint, but beyond that they knew very little.

His own former fiancée had been more intelligent than the average lady, but also very vain about her looks and her station. She was after all a duke's daughter. It was her right to be.

Or so Nicholas had thought at the time. But since becoming reacquainted with the vicar's daughter, he realized how shallow his former fiancée now seemed.

As guilty as he felt about it, he was sorely glad he would not have to marry Lady Katherine Montbatten.

His thoughts were broken when Christina came toward him. "I see you are getting acquainted with Ty, and look, he's even smiling!" she cried as she smoothed her hand over his downy head.

Nicholas had trouble forming a response with her standing so close to him. She smelled like honeysuckle, and he found himself wanting to kiss her.

"I knew he would like you!"

He blinked and made himself get control of his wayward thoughts. Clearing his throat, he finally spoke. "If he likes me, he has a strange way of showing it. He was screaming the chandeliers down until you walked in here."

Just as he thought she might, Christina laughed at his dry words. She looked up at him and their eyes met. A strange feeling came over Nicholas as he stared into those laughing eyes. There they were, the two of them, standing together with a baby between them. If anyone had walked into the room at that moment, they would have thought they came upon a couple of proud parents with their newborn son—family.

Something, Nicholas had convinced himself, that would never be a part of his future.

He was allowing this snip of a girl to lure him into thinking he could be happy. That he could be. . .normal.

But he wasn't. He, the scoundrel and wastrel who had brought pain to his family and dishonor to his friends.

Christina believed that God loved him no matter what he had done. But Nicholas knew that even God could not forgive him.

How could He when Nicholas could not forgive himself?

Pushing the infant into Christina's surprised arms, he mumbled something about making an appointment with his steward and walked out as quickly as his injured leg would allow him to.

❧

Christina watched with concerned eyes as the earl made a mad dash to the door, as if wild boars were nipping at his heels. For a moment, he had seemed more open than ever.

But when their eyes had met and held for a few breathtaking seconds, she'd watched his expression change, as if a door suddenly closed on his happiness. All that remained was a face full of self-loathing, and Christina was positive she'd also seen fear.

Sighing, she kissed Ty's head before looking over at Mrs. Sanborne. The older woman was staring at the door with a confused look upon her usually smiling face.

"I'd hoped he would stay longer," she murmured before turning her gaze to Christina. "Do you suppose it was because I pushed him into holding the baby? I just thought that if he could hold the child, he might feel a bond or *something*."

Christina went to the woman and put a comforting hand on her arm. "It is not your fault, Mrs. Sanborne. It's just going to take a little time before Lord Thornton adjusts to having a baby around."

The nanny smiled at her. "I suppose you're right." She reached out for the baby. "I'll just take Ty up to the nursery and put him down for his nap."

She left Christina alone in the library. Once she was out of sight, Christina headed for the east wing of the estate. She'd discovered a few days earlier that this particular wing of the hall had not been used for years. All the furniture was covered and cobwebs hung thickly from the chandeliers and corners of the massive rooms.

It wasn't a strange thing for some of the hall not to be in use. Many titled families used only a small portion of their grand homes, some because of a lack of money and others because they didn't want to be bothered. Since Christina knew the Thorntons were one of the wealthiest families in England, she knew the reason for the neglect had to be the latter.

A shiver snaked up her back as she walked through the cool, darkened hallways, guided by the light of a single candle. She was glad to finally reach her destination.

The enormous carved door creaked as Christina pushed it open. Inside, Helen sat staring wide-eyed and apparently frightened out of her wits in the middle of an immense room, holding the crate of puppies.

Christina gasped in awe as she stepped into the grand ballroom, still beautiful even after years of neglect and busy spiders. Helen had thrown the heavy curtains back, and sunlight warmed the otherwise cool, damp room.

"Are you sure we won't be discovered here?" Helen asked anxiously as Christina set about removing the milk she'd brought from her house.

"Of course I'm sure. I asked Pierce the best place to keep them, and he recommended this wing of the mansion. He also assured me no one ever comes here."

Helen let out a gasp of dismay. "You told Pierce!"

Christina dipped the edge of a rag into the milk, preparing to feed the puppies. "I had to ask someone, Helen. Besides, he told me he is indebted to me for the tonic I mixed up for him to get rid of the fleas on his cat. Our secret is quite safe."

And it seemed it would remain so since the night passed and the earl was still none the wiser. Pierce had even lit a fire in the huge fireplace to keep the pups warm and made sure they were fed first thing the next morning.

"I've grown quite fond of the little spotted one, Miss. I fear I shall insist on bringing him home to the missus when he's old enough," Pierce confided to Christina when she arrived midmorning. She'd worried all night over the puppies' health and safety, but apparently it was all for naught. Pierce had turned out to be quite the guardian.

"Of course you shall have him. That just leaves the other

five to worry about!" she exclaimed with exaggeration.

"Don't you worry about a thing, Miss. I'll inquire around to see if anyone is interested," he assured her.

"Interested in what?" a deep voice spoke behind them.

Christina slowly turned to Lord Thornton, searching his face for clues to how much he'd heard of their conversation. Pierce saved the day.

"Ah. I see you've decided to come down for breakfast, my lord. I'll send word to Cook that you'll be joining Miss Wakelin," he said in his usual emotionless manner as he headed toward the kitchens.

"But I didn't want breakfast," the earl said, but by that time, Pierce was already out of the room.

He turned his irate gaze to Christina, who put up a hand, shaking her head. "Don't look at me. I've already had my breakfast!"

Thornton sighed in frustration. "I've become convinced I should fire my whole household and hire new servants. It seems lately they all do the opposite of what I want at every turn!"

Christina had to smile at his exasperated tone. Despite his words, he actually seemed happier than she'd ever seen him. His countenance wasn't dark and brooding as it was when she'd first met him. Just the fact that he was walking about and not hibernating in his chambers proved that a slight change was happening inside him.

"Most of them have been here at Kenswick since you were a young boy. Perhaps they are just trying to look after you the best they know how."

He brought his gaze back to her. "I don't need or want to be looked after."

Christina let her eyes roam over Nicholas Thornton's incredibly handsome features. It was true he presented a picture of a man who needed no one, but she could feel the sadness and loneliness radiating from him. He needed someone to look after him worse than anybody she'd ever known. He just didn't know it.

She would need God's guidance in how to help him realize it.

"Breakfast is served!" Pierce announced from the doorway and just as quickly disappeared again.

"It would seem the matter of wanting or needing to be looked after has been taken out of your hands," she told the earl with a grin.

The brooding Earl of Kenswick actually returned her smile, although sheepishly. "You could be right. Or Pierce could be using breakfast as an excuse to check up on you, since you seem to be alone in my presence without your chaperone about."

He held out his arm and with a raised eyebrow asked with mock formality, "Miss Wakelin, will you be so kind as to allow me to escort you to the morning room?"

Christina laughed softly as she put her hand on his arm. She knew she needed to see about the puppies, but she could not turn down his offer. He was in such a different mood that she felt drawn to him like never before. "Indeed, I shall," she answered, matching his tone, and together they went into the morning room.

He stayed in that pleasant mood all through breakfast, even after he noticed Pierce standing just inside the room to act as a chaperone. He merely nodded to the man, then took a big bite of the sticky bun on his plate. Only once did

Lord Thornton mention hearing a strange noise in the night that sounded like animal cries. Christina offered him some more marmalade to distract him, and that seemed to do the trick. He mentioned the cries no more.

In fact, Christina realized it was surprisingly easy to get the earl to forget he'd asked a question. If she thought it a little odd, she dismissed the thought as soon as it entered her mind. Why worry over nothing?

seven

Of course, Nicholas was not so easily distracted, nor was he a simpleton. He knew when something was being pulled over his eyes; he just didn't know what, exactly, that something was.

He spent all day thinking about it and finally came to the conclusion that Christina must have brought some sort of animal into the house. Pierce was evidently in on it since he'd been avoiding him all day.

Whatever it was, he hoped it wouldn't eat his cat.

But that was not the only thing preying on his mind. Right before Christina left in the afternoon, she'd casually invited him to church the next day.

He'd acted like a stiff-necked buffoon! He'd grown defensive, and instead of declining like a gentleman, he'd answered with a cold no and quickly left the room. He didn't know how to explain that going to church scared him. People expected things out of you when they saw you in church. They expected you to act more like a Christian should, being kind and giving to others.

Nicholas knew he had not been a kind man in many years, and the only thing he'd given to anybody was a lot of grief and pain.

No. Going to church would make everyone expect him to change, and he just didn't know how to do that.

No matter how much he wished it were so.

No matter how much he wanted to show Christina he could.

❧

Christina had no appetite as she sat down to dinner with her father that evening. If only she could have waited before blurting out such an invitation. The earl was just beginning to open up to her, and she had to go and ruin it by issuing an invitation to church too soon.

It was obvious he wasn't ready to discuss God yet, and she'd pushed too hard. If only she had her father's way of speaking to people. He had such a soothing manner even the angriest man could be calmed with just a few spoken words from the vicar.

"You've hardly touched your stew, Daughter, and you know how Cook gets offended if you leave too much uneaten," her father teased, pulling her from her melancholy mood.

Christina managed to give him a small smile. "I'm sorry, Father. It's just that I think I made the earl upset today when I invited him to church, and I feel awful about it." She absently pushed the vegetables around in her bowl.

She looked up to find her father's worried eyes studying her carefully. "You have not taken a fancy to the earl, have you, Christina? You do spend quite a bit of time at Kenswick Hall these days."

Christina knew she could not lie to her father, but neither could she tell him the truth. "I only see the earl a couple of times a day, Papa. Most of the time I am with Helen, Mrs. Sanborne, and Ty," she carefully evaded. "It's just that I know if he could hear one of your sermons, he would feel so much better."

The vicar shook his head. "Christina, one sermon is not going to fix what ails the Earl of Kenswick. God can change him, yes, but only if he allows Him to."

An idea began to form in Christina's mind. "What if you go and speak to him, Papa? From what I've gathered from the things he's said and what I've been told from the servants, he blames himself for his father's death. I also think he feels guilty for his behavior after he returned from the war." She pushed her bowl back and reached for her father's hand. "If you could speak to him, it might help him."

The vicar studied his daughter a moment before nodding his head reluctantly. "I will go, but I cannot promise anything. My concern, however, is more for you than for him. You must promise me you will not fill your head with any silly notions of romance between you and Lord Thornton. Even if he did not have the reputation he had or the problems surrounding him, he would still be completely out of our class. Earls do not marry vicars' daughters, Christina. You must remember that."

Christina knew all this, of course. Hadn't she told herself the very same thing from the moment she'd fallen into his arms? Yet hearing her father say it so bluntly hurt just the same. "I harbor no such aspirations of being the Earl of Kenswick's wife, Papa. I am twenty-three and already past the age of desirability for a bride from even a man of my own station. Your fears are completely unjustified."

Her words, meant to calm, had just the opposite effect on her father. "You speak as though you have resigned to being an old maid! That is ridiculous, Christina. There are many young men in our acquaintance who have shown interest in you. You are much too lovely to be put on the shelf, and I will not have you speak so!"

Christina smiled at his disgruntled expression. "I am lovely only to you, Papa. To those young men you speak of, I'm merely the strange vicar's daughter who spends too much time with animals and speaks her own mind too often."

"Then you must learn to control your tongue and spend more time indoors!" he declared, but Christina saw that he looked a little sheepish at the ridiculous statement. "What I mean is, you must show them the part of you I love so much—the loving, caring girl who would give away her own food before seeing even her enemy starve."

Christina rose from her seat and bent to kiss her father's bald, shiny head. "I will endeavor to appear more loveable in the future, Papa. I promise. Before you know it, all of Derbyshire will be lined up at our door asking for my hand!"

The vicar chuckled and playfully swatted her away. "Perhaps it's the earl I should be concerned about! You may end up causing the chap more problems than he already has."

❧

The next morning, Nicholas knew right off it was not going to be a pleasant day. He had leftover guilt for turning down Christina's invitation, and he'd berated himself half the night for allowing himself to *feel* the guilt. What was wrong with him that her downcast expression would bother him so?

But that wasn't his only aggravation.

It was Sunday. Everyone in his household knew on Sunday he slept late, had his breakfast late, and then spent the entire day in his workshop, working on his carvings. Why his servants collectively forgot about this schedule was beyond his understanding.

He wondered if a mutiny were afoot, and if so, who was the leader?

It certainly wasn't his unwanted, yet still employed, valet, although he did a good job of beginning his Sunday on the wrong foot.

Smith had awakened him at seven and all but shoved him into a dark blue coat, dove gray vest, and britches. He was tugging on his black Hessians before he had the wits to inquire why he was wearing one of his finer suits.

"You'll want to look your best when you attend the service this morning, my lord," Smith answered as if his going was a foregone conclusion.

A vessel started to pulse in his temple. "I beg your pardon, but in the very short time you've been here, have you ever known me to get up and attend church?" he barked while running a hand through his hair in frustration.

Smith seemed oblivious to his disgruntled attitude, however, as he rummaged about the room, picking up Nicholas's bedclothes. "Ah, but Miss Wakelin had never invited you before yesterday, my lord."

"But I told her I would—" He stopped as something occurred to him. "How could you possibly know she even asked me? I don't remember you being there, Smith!"

Smith threw Nicholas an absent smile as he continued to busy himself about the room. "Oh, I wasn't, Sir, but although it's not something you like to acknowledge, we servants do talk, my lord."

He knew Christina would never say anything, and, besides, she wasn't a servant. Young Ty could do nothing but emit baby sounds, so that left only one person. "Mrs. Sanborne! I'll fire her, posthaste!"

"That wouldn't be wise, my lord. You'd be left with a baby you have no idea how to care for. Miss Wakelin would probably stop coming by because she'd be upset you dismissed a lady she's grown quite fond of, and the solitude you crave so mightily would be turned topsy-turvy."

Nicholas stared in amazement at the man who had insinuated himself into his life and household. "I'm all agog at your reasoning, Smith. It almost sounds a little like blackmail."

Smith bowed to Nicholas. "I would never presume to resort to blackmailing, your lordship." With that he turned and walked to the bedroom door. "I'll inform Cook you'll be down in a moment." He offered another brief bow before leaving the room.

Stunned that he'd been hoodwinked yet again by his wily valet, it took a few seconds for Nicholas to respond. "I will eat breakfast, but I will not be attending church!" he shouted at the closed door, knowing Smith would probably not hear him.

He managed to get through breakfast without mishap and conveyed to Smith, Pierce, and any other servant within earshot that he was definitely *not* leaving the house.

But the moment he finished breakfast, Mrs. Sanborne breezed into the dining room and pushed his nephew into his arms. "I'm terribly sorry, my lord, but I fear I cannot look after Master Ty today. I just received a terribly frightening note from my daughter's husband. She's gone into labor with her first child, and she's terribly afraid and needs me there with her. I'm sure you understand, do you not, my lord?"

Nicholas opened his mouth to say he very much did not understand, when she rushed ahead of him. "That's terribly good of you, Lord Thornton. Terribly good."

Nicholas looked down at his nephew with dismay. "But, Mrs. Sanborne, you cannot leave me. . . ." He stopped when he looked up and realized she'd already left the room.

He ran to catch her, but no amount of pleading or threats of termination would induce her to stay.

Nicholas was so perplexed that he stood out on the front steps of the hall for ten minutes after her carriage pulled away.

How was a person to know what babies wanted or needed? Were there instructions written down somewhere he could follow? His housekeeper had left the estate for some purpose or another. Not knowing what else to do, he went to the nursery and sat in the high-backed rocking chair.

So there he was, the sixth Earl of Kenswick, doing something he was sure none of his forebears had ever done—rocking an infant. For five minutes or so, he fumed about the circumstances he found himself in. As he rocked back and forth, he promised himself he would add more servants to his small staff. With that settled in his mind, he calmed down a little and for the first time really noticed the baby in his arms.

He did look so much like his brother. So much so it hurt a little to hold him, knowing his brother never would. And then he thought of something else: What would it be like to hold his own son?

Of course, that wasn't a possibility for him, and it irritated him that he would even entertain such thoughts.

Christina. Christina Wakelin was the reason his priorities were so confused. His was a well-ordered solitary world until she came into his life.

The baby made a noise. Nicholas looked down at him, panicked that he was about to cry. What would he do then? There was no one to hand him to! But little Ty didn't cry. Instead, he looked up at Nicholas with a full gaze. A warm feeling spread throughout the earl's body, and an unfamiliar emotion squeezed at his heart as he studied the child. He might have determined never to marry and have children, but someone (God?) had seen fit to give him a child anyway.

What was next, a wife? Immediately, Christina Wakelin's teasing smile and shiny auburn hair flashed into his mind's eye. That shook him up more than any thought of children did.

She was the kind of woman who would brighten a man's life and fill his home with laughter and love. It would certainly not be a boring life with her in it!

If only he were a different man. If only. . .

"My lord, Reverend Wakelin is here to see you," Pierce announced at the nursery's door. "I've shown him to the parlor."

Nicholas opened his mouth to reply that he was not receiving visitors, but changed his mind when the baby started to make fussing noises. Seizing the opportunity, he quickly got up from the rocker and placed the baby into Pierce's arms.

"You don't mind seeing to the baby while I greet the vicar, do you, Pierce?" He gave the surprised man a triumphant smile. "Of course, you don't," he answered for him as he slipped out of the room.

As Nicholas entered the parlor, he made a quick study of Christina's father. He'd aged, of course, since the last time he'd seen him, but he still was the tall, stately looking man he'd always been. There was a kindness in the vicar's eyes that had always warmed him as a child, listening to the Sunday sermons.

The vicar stood with a welcoming smile as he gave a brief bow to Nicholas. "Lord Thornton," he greeted. "It's been quite a few years since we last met."

Nicholas returned the smile, though a bit warily. What could the vicar possibly want, and did Christina have anything to do with it?

"It has indeed, Reverend. Please have a seat," he directed, indicating the brocade-covered chairs near the massive marble fireplace. "To what do I owe the pleasure of your company?" he asked once they were seated.

"There's no need to pretend you are overjoyed to have me intrude on your time," the vicar stated dryly, though a kind grin lit his face. "Christina has spoken to me a little of what you've gone through these last few weeks, and may I start off by saying I am truly sorry for the loss of both your father and your brother. Your father was one of my dearest friends, and I still miss him terribly."

Nicholas nodded. "As do I, Reverend." He hesitated but found he had to ask, "So Christina asked you to come speak to me? I know she must be upset that I did not attend the services, but I—"

Reverend Wakelin held up his hand to stop the explanation. "Yes, she did ask me to come, but that is not why I agreed." He leaned forward, resting his elbows on his knees and looking seriously into Nicholas's eyes. "She wanted me to come and speak to you as your vicar, but I'm afraid I came as someone else. Christina's father."

Nicholas took a deep breath as he absorbed the vicar's words. Of course, he should have seen this coming. "I see,"

Nicholas said. "You think I might have had ulterior motives in asking Christina to help me."

Reverend Wakelin wasn't a man to beat around the bush. "That is it exactly."

"Then let me set your mind at ease, Reverend. Christina is completely safe in this household. I would never do anything to jeopardize her reputation."

"I'm afraid you already have," the vicar answered.

eight

That got Nicholas's attention. "I beg your pardon?"

"You have jeopardized Christina's reputation, and if it weren't for the fact they all know Christina well and love her as their own kin, it wouldn't just be jeopardized, it would be ruined." Reverend Wakelin took a deep breath and continued. "She is a young, unmarried woman, and you, Sir, do not have the best reputation. Now, I am not one to listen to or believe gossip, but there is so much scandal attached to your name that I fear it can't all be just speculation. My parishioners are afraid you might have the power to lead her astray."

At those accusing words, Nicholas stiffened. "While it is true I have done things for which I am extremely ashamed of, Sir, I would never do anything to harm Miss Wakelin. She has been too kind in her efforts to help me. I would not see her name sullied." He swallowed, looking away from the vicar's piercing gaze.

"Then there's only one thing to do," the vicar stated.

Nicholas's head snapped back toward the tall man across from him. "You want me to marry her! That is what all this is leading to, is it not? You feel I have compromised her, so I need to offer to make it right!"

"I should say not!" the vicar all but shouted at him, causing Nicholas to sit back in surprise. "Christina is much too carefree to be thrust into the life of a countess. I would see her married to a nice farmer or small land-holder, not to the aristocracy! She would never fit."

The reasonable part of Nicholas agreed with the vicar that, indeed, she would be better suited to a simpler life. But another part of the earl was captivated by the thought of Christina being his bride. She'd brought so many changes to his life in the short time since he'd found her in his tree. And with the changes had come laughter and brightness to his dark world. He'd come to rely on her goodness even though he pretended he didn't want it.

What would it be like to have Christina as a wife?

But as he turned his eyes back to the serious stare of the vicar, he knew marrying Christina would never be possible. They not only came from two different social classes, she was much too naïve and innocent, whereas he, sadly, was not.

"Of course, you are right. I apologize for jumping to such an erroneous conclusion," he answered.

The vicar smiled slightly as if he'd glimpsed what was going through Nicholas's head. "No harm done. I was merely going to say she must continue to have Helen as a chaperone, and you must never be seen together in public."

"Of course," he agreed. "As for the latter, haven't you heard, Reverend? I never leave the estate."

The vicar nodded, but if Nicholas thought this was the end of their conversation, he was mistaken. "Now that we have the subject of my daughter out of the way, I would like to ask you something about yourself."

Nicholas sighed, leaning back in his chair and throwing up his arms in surrender. "Of course you may ask, though I'm sure there's little you and the rest of England do not already know."

"I want to know how long you intend to hang onto the guilt that has taken over your life."

A shadow fell over Nicholas's face. He did not like the personal turn this conversation had taken. "Guilt?"

"Your father was ill long before you returned from the war and broke your engagement, you know. Several times I visited and prayed with him when he'd had an episode with his heart."

"But it was my bad behavior that pushed him over the edge, Reverend. I know it was!" Nicholas said harshly, his fists clenched on the arms of the chair.

"Do you not think he knew what the war had done to you? He saw the pain you endured with your leg; he knew the images of battle haunted your every dream and thought. We spoke of it and prayed that God would see you through it," the vicar tried to explain, but Nicholas would not believe it.

"Yet all God did was take my father from me!" Nicholas growled as he stood and limped to the window, which he now kept opened because of Christina. He deliberately put extra pressure on his leg so he could feel the pain and be reminded of why he'd made the choices he had.

The vicar stood and turned to where the earl was. "It was your father's time to go, and he was ready for it. His dying wish was to see you happy once again, to have God heal all the bitterness war had put in your heart."

Nicholas turned to look at Reverend Wakelin, his face ravaged by pain. "How can God heal a heart that is no longer there?"

Reverend Wakelin gazed at Nicholas with compassion. "It is there, my lord, it's just that it has been broken. You must allow God to mend it back together. He loves you, you know. Even after all you've done, God still loves you."

A tiny spark of hope flickered in Nicholas's heart when he heard those words, yet he was afraid to believe them. "I will think on all you have told me, Reverend. Thank you for coming by," he said by way of a dismissal. He didn't want to be rude to Christina's father, but he needed to be alone.

The vicar seemed to understand. He nodded to Nicholas. "I bid you good day, my lord."

Nicholas must have stood looking out his window for an hour after the vicar left. And it might have been longer had he not heard a strange whimpering sound. At first he thought it might be his nephew, but as he listened closer, he realized it was the same strange sound he'd heard before. What in the world was it?

Nicholas moved down the hall following the sound until he came to the closed door that led to the east wing. He stood close to the door and decided the sound was definitely coming from that particular wing.

Nicholas frowned. That wing hadn't been used since his mother died years before. Had a wild animal somehow gotten into the house?

He was just about to open the door to check it out when Pierce, still holding the baby, swaddled in a blanket, came seemingly out of nowhere. He acted quite nervous as he positioned himself between Nicholas and the door. "Ah, here you are, my lord. I've been looking for you."

Nicholas's black brow rose as he studied his butler curiously. "Well, you have found me. What was it you wanted?"

Pierce tugged at his collar. "Wanted? Yes. . .well, I. . .needed to tell you something!"

Nicholas sighed, "Of course. You want me to take Ty," he surmised as he held out his arms.

Pierce stepped away from him with a quick shake of his head. "Oh, no! Master Ty is doing quite all right on my shoulder. We wouldn't want to wake him by moving him about." He gave the infant a gentle pat on his back.

Nicholas waited for more, but when Pierce merely stood there staring at him, he prompted, "If the baby wasn't the reason you wanted to see me, then what was?"

"Oh, of course, my lord! I was to tell you that Cook is preparing rabbit stew for tonight's meal."

Nicholas stared at his butler and wondered if poor old Pierce was working too hard lately. He knew good and well Nicholas couldn't care less about the menu.

Making a mental note to give the man more time off, Nicholas nodded slowly. "That's fine, Pierce. Now if you'll move, I will be able to open this door and enter the east wing."

Pierce didn't budge. "Oh, you don't want to venture into that wing, Sir."

Nicholas was fast losing patience. "And why wouldn't I?"

"It's drafty, my lord. Very drafty."

"I think I can handle it, so please move."

"But, my lord. . ."

The butler's words faded as he realized Nicholas was going to get his way no matter what he said. With reluctance, he moved to the side.

As Nicholas opened the door, the musty smell of the unused rooms assaulted his senses. Just as Pierce had predicted, the hall was quite drafty.

The mewing animal sound grew louder. And did he hear the faint sound of voices? Odd.

"My lord, I beg you to rethink—" Pierce attempted one more time to stop him, but Nicholas interrupted.

"I don't know what you're trying to hide from me, Pierce, but I'm going to find out," he stated firmly as he started down the dim hallway.

He heard a nervous "Oh, dear" from his butler, but Nicholas didn't stop as he made his way closer to where the sound was coming from.

When he reached the old ballroom and stuck his head inside, he saw Christina and Helen sitting in the middle of the room, playing with a litter of puppies.

"What are you doing in here?" he asked, his voice sounding harsher than he had intended. But a part of him was irritated she hadn't told him about the puppies. Why did she feel she had to hide them from him? She had evidently even told his butler.

Both young women turned toward him, their eyes wide with surprise at having been caught.

Helen was the first to respond. "Ooohhh, I knew this would happen! Did I not tell you we would be caught, Christina!" She cast a frightened look toward Nicholas. "Please, have mercy on us, my lord. I pray you will not deal harshly because of our harboring these puppies in your ballroom!" She clasped her hands to her chest in a melodramatic fashion.

Nicholas stood nonplussed for a moment, staring at her as if she'd lost her mind. He turned his gaze to Christina, wondering if she suffered from the same hysterics as her friend.

Apparently not, because the woman was actually grinning at him.

"Please excuse Helen, Lord Thornton. She's quite convinced, because you've fought two duels, that you are capable of any manner of dastardly behavior." She reached over to pat her friend on the arm. "She also reads the occasional gothic romance, and so her imagination tends toward the spectacular."

Nicholas walked toward the women, ignoring the way Helen shrank back as he drew closer. "And what do you think, Miss Wakelin? Did you think I might have the puppies tossed into the lake if you told me about them?"

Christina frowned at his words. "No," she answered slowly, as if choosing her words carefully. "I merely thought you would refuse to let me keep the puppies here at Kenswick Hall."

"When have I refused you anything that you were able to contrive in the end?"

The frown disappeared and her sunny smile was back in place, much to Nicholas's pleasure. "Excellent point, my lord!" She held up a little black and white puppy for him to see. "Now that you know our little secret, why don't you take a look at our babies? Aren't they beautiful?"

Beautiful wasn't the word Nicholas would have used, but he didn't say so. The pups looked to be a mixture of collie and something unidentifiable. But judging by the large paws on the creatures, he had a feeling that something else was not a small breed.

He stooped down to where they sat, his gaze drawn to Christina. For one breathless moment, he stared at her, wondering what his life would be like if her father had demanded he marry her. Perhaps she would be able to help him as she wanted to do. Perhaps she could bring light into his dark world.

But then what would her life be like? Would she resent

being forced to marry him? Would she become like he was—bitter, lost, even angry? Christina Wakelin did not deserve to be shackled to someone like him. She deserved so much better.

Deliberately, he broke eye contact, and in the process his gaze lit on Helen. No longer was her expression fearful; instead, her eyes narrowed with speculation.

What did the little busybody see? Was his attraction for Christina obvious? Surely not. He was always careful to keep his face blank—a trick he'd found useful while leading his troops in the war. Whatever was going through her mind was just as Christina had suggested—the product of an overactive imagination.

"This room is too drafty for the puppies," he stated, seizing on the first thing that came to his mind. "Why don't we take them down to the stables? The hay will keep them nice and warm, and Miles, my head groomsman, can look after them when you are not here."

He saw the wondering look that passed between them as he picked up the box and led them out of the ballroom.

"I missed you at church, my lord," Christina said, her voice sounding nonchalant. "I had high hopes you would be able to see my father. Whenever he speaks of you, there is a fondness in his voice, you know."

Nicholas had trouble believing that statement. "No need to fear, Miss Wakelin. Your father saw fit to bring his 'fond' voice over to Kenswick Hall this afternoon and pay me a visit," he replied dryly as he reached the door that led outside to the stables. "Would you be so kind as to open the door for me? I seem to have my hands full at the moment."

Christina stared blankly at him for a moment until Helen gave her a nudge. "What? Oh! Yes, let me get that," she mumbled, pushing at the heavy door.

But when they had stepped outside, she said, "I'm sorry, but did I just hear you say my father paid you a visit?"

Nicholas threw her a mocking glance. "Why do you act surprised? Did you not send him yourself?"

She shook her head. "I did ask him to come, but he would not give me an answer. I had no idea he would actually pay you a visit!"

Not quite knowing if he believed her or not, Nicholas stepped around her, resuming his trek to the stable. "Well, he did."

"But. . .wait!"

Nicholas glanced back to find Christina running to catch up to him. He also noticed Helen had not followed them inside the stable.

Recalling the vicar's words of warning, Nicholas said, "You better go back and fetch your friend. One of the promises your father extracted from me was that I would not be in your presence without a chaperone."

Christina stopped just short of running into him, causing them to be no more than a few inches apart.

"Oh, no!" she cried, putting a hand to her cheek. "I wanted him to talk to you about God, but he came to warn you to stay away from me, didn't he!"

"Not exactly, but he was concerned for your reputation; and I fully agree, Miss Wakelin. I would not see your good name sullied because of me." He turned and set the box down in the first empty stall he came to.

She followed him. "If I am fodder for the town gossips,

then it is no one's fault but my own. It is my choice to come here, and Papa should not have said anything to you. Please don't let yourself feel responsible for my reputation."

Nicholas stared down into her beautiful eyes and wondered about the emotion he saw in them. She looked at him as if she cared a great deal about him. But surely he was mistaken. She had said herself that she came to Kenswick Hall because she'd made it her mission to help him believe in God again. That was all he was to her—just a lost soul in need of guidance.

"What are you doing here, Christina?" he murmured, not realizing he'd used her Christian name. "Why aren't you being courted by some nice farmer who will give you a home and pretty babies of your own?"

She laughed lightly. "Now I know you've been talking to Papa! If he has said that once, he's said it a thousand times!"

Nicholas didn't laugh, nor did he smile. "He's right, you know. There is no reason why you should not leave this place and never return."

He'd hoped his words would drive her away for her own sake. But as usual she appeared undaunted. "There is every reason, my lord. You need me here, and so does young Ty. For the first time in my life, I feel as though I'm doing something worthwhile, something greater than nursing sick animals or acting as hostess to my father's congregation."

Her words filled him with an emotion he was afraid to name. They were like a healing balm to his heart, yet still he felt so undeserving.

"Do you know that when he started speaking of your reputation, I thought he was here to demand satisfaction," he said.

Christina looked puzzled. "You mean a duel?"

He grinned, shaking his head. "No, I mean marriage."

"And you told this to my father?" she said, trying not to laugh.

Nicholas could see nothing funny about it. "Yes," he answered stiffly.

More laughter. "You must give us more credit than that, my lord," she replied.

"Miss Wakelin, I'm at a loss to see what's so funny about me believing your father was demanding that I do right by you. It is a natural summation!"

She managed to stop laughing, but she could not seem to stop grinning at him.

"You are a peer. I am a vicar's daughter. To suppose you would marry so far beneath you, no matter what the reason, would be quite foolish on my father's part," she said. Then, turning away from him, she walked out of the stable. "Fear not, my lord! Your bachelorhood is quite safe where I'm concerned," she called over her shoulder, the laughter still ringing in her voice.

In three long steps, Nicholas had her by the arm, pulling her around to face him. "Do you think I'm such a cad that I would not do right by a woman?"

She smiled up at him, and he wished he could understand the emotion behind her eyes. "Of course not. But I am aware of my place in society, as I am sure you are also."

An odd feeling rushed through Nicholas's mind and heart. It made him want to deny her words, rebel against a society that would make a beautiful girl like Christina think she could not win any man's heart, no matter what her station in life.

It was that feeling that compelled him to say, "If you are aware, Miss Wakelin, I am not exactly in society's favor. And, frankly, even if I were, I would not let them be a factor when I chose the woman I would marry."

"Then you have changed your mind about living the rest of your days in bitter solitude?" she asked.

It struck Nicholas that hiding himself away from society was no longer appealing. He no longer wanted to lick his wounds and live within the bitter darkness he'd enveloped himself in.

No. Not since Christina Wakelin, the vicar's daughter, had dared to climb his tree.

And had dared to tell him she could never be a suitable match for him.

"Perhaps I have changed my mind after all," he murmured with a secretive smile.

nine

"What is wrong with the earl?" Helen asked for the fourth time as they strolled along the path that led into town.

Indeed, Christina concurred silently, *what* was *wrong with the earl?* To Helen she merely feigned ignorance. "I don't know what you mean."

Helen threw her an incredulous look. "You must know what I'm talking about! For the last week, a transformation has occurred. He is no longer glaring at us or hiding in his study. He has actually been smiling, Christina, and has become a permanent fixture in whatever room we are in." She stepped in front of Christina and put her hands on Christina's arms. "You must see that this behavior is highly unusual and quite disturbing."

Christina sighed. "All right, I do admit he is acting rather strangely, but I wouldn't call it disturbing, nor do I mind the change. Perhaps he is beginning to heal from all that has happened to him. I believe having his nephew in his life has made him see that life is too important to hide from."

Helen shook her head, causing her ringlets to bob like dangled sausages about her head. "I do not believe it is his nephew that has wrought this change, Christina. I believe it is because of you."

Christina studied her friend's grave countenance. "Helen, I don't think. . ."

"I believe the earl has developed affections for you of a most romantic nature!" Helen blurted.

If only it were so, Christina thought. But she knew better. "Perhaps he's beginning to realize he cannot keep himself shut off from the world. I'm sure it is for his nephew's sake that he is coming about."

Helen started to argue the point when the biggest gossip in Malbury, Mrs. Blaylock, caught sight of them as she stepped out of one of the little shops along the way. She was dressed in her usual colorful, flamboyant style, today wearing a taffeta dress of green and pink stripes. Upon her head she wore an elaborate turban of the same fabric with a bright peacock feather sprouting up in the front.

"Oh, dear," Christina whispered to Helen. "She's headed this way as if she's on a mission."

"Perhaps it's to tell us where in all of England you can actually purchase that particular green and pink striped fabric. Do you think she has it specially made?" Helen whispered back.

"Hmm," was all Christina could reply, for Mrs. Blaylock had already reached them.

"Why, good morning, Mrs. Blaylock! God has surely favored us with a beautiful sunny day, has He not?" Christina sang out with her usual cheery smile, as both she and Helen bobbed a quick curtsy.

"Indeed He has," Mrs. Blaylock returned, although her smile was more calculating than pleasant. "It has also been an informative one."

By the way the woman looked at her, Christina had a sinking feeling that her information had something to do with her going to Kenswick Hall every day. "Well, that's wonderful, Mrs. Blaylock. Now, if you'll excuse us, we really have to be—"

"Yes, indeed. When I saw his lordship, I couldn't understand what he was doing in town, but now that I've run into you, why it all makes perfect sense," she interrupted, her peacock feather bobbing up and down as she talked.

Christina was so shocked at hearing Lord Thornton was strolling about Malbury that the insinuation flew right past her. "You're joking! Are you sure it was he?" she exclaimed.

"Come, come, Miss Wakelin. There's no need for pretense. We are friends and neighbors after all."

This time there was no misunderstanding.

And this woman was no friend.

"I can assure you, Mrs. Blaylock, I had no idea that Lord Thornton would be in town, but I'll admit I am happily surprised. Since losing his father and brother, he has let sadness overwhelm him," she said coolly to the busybody. "So I'm sure you'll agree it is indeed a blessing from God to see his heartbreak mending enough for him to be able to face society once again."

Christina should have known a mild set-down would not deter her. "Or perhaps it is because you have spent so much time with him, that he is making a fast recovery."

"Indeed, I know that cannot be correct. I've spent time only with his nephew and rarely with Lord Thornton."

"And then only with me as her chaperone!" Helen interjected in a surprising show of boldness. Usually her friend ran from confrontations.

Mrs. Blaylock, while not looking fully convinced, knew she would not get the information she wanted to hear. "It never entered my mind that you would have been without a chaperone," the gossiper said with mock innocence.

"We really should get that book your father wanted before the noon hour, Christina," Helen broke in, and Christina quickly seized the lifeline her friend had thrown her.

"You are right. Good day, Madam. I trust we'll see you at church on Sunday?"

"As always," the woman replied as she swept past them, leaving a wake of oversweet perfume.

As they continued on into town, Helen voiced her concern. "I do not like this, Christina. She could hurt your reputation with her speculations about you and the earl!"

"Nonsense, Helen. Anything that woman says is of no consequence, and everyone in Malbury knows it." Christina didn't know what it mattered anyway. She never had a single offer for her hand, and there seemed to be no prospects looming over the horizon. If she were doomed to be an old maid, she'd rather be an interesting one!

They spent about ten minutes in the bookstore and purchased the book her father had asked for. Just as they stepped out of the store, Jane Phillips and her mother joined them. While Jane was a sweet, friendly girl, her mother was quite the opposite, especially since her husband had been knighted. This elevated station, in Mrs. Phillips's mind, put them above their country neighbors, and she never let anyone forget about it.

They greeted Jane and Mrs. Phillips, and before they could say another word, Mrs. Phillips said, "I don't suppose you ladies have heard the news?"

"You'll never guess who has been seen riding through town!" Jane blurted.

"Don't gush, Dear. It's so unbecoming," her mother scolded.

Jane, standing in front of her mother, rolled her eyes in exasperation, as Christina answered, "Yes, we have heard Lord Thornton was seen about town this morning."

For a moment Mrs. Phillips just stared at Christina blankly. "My word, I did not know that particular bit of news. No, no, Dear. Something much more exciting."

"It was the Duke of Northingshire. Oh, we saw his grand black coach with a stunningly painted ducal crest on either side. And most amazing of all was that it was seen going toward Kenswick Hall!"

"I hear his grace has beautiful estates in both England and Scotland," Helen commented, and Christina had no doubt it was true. Helen was so fascinated with the nobles that she hoarded every word printed or said about them. She probably knew more about these strangers than she did about the members of her own family!

"Of course he has extensive estates, my dear. He is one of the wealthiest dukes in all of England," Mrs. Phillips added, not to be outdone. She then turned her gaze to Christina. "I hear you have become acquainted with Lord Thornton recently. Perhaps you might know the nature of his grace's visit."

"I have only assisted with the earl's nephew and his nanny. I would not know anything about a visit from the Duke of Northingshire," Christina replied, silently adding, *and I bet Lord Thornton doesn't know either!*

Mrs. Phillips smiled haughtily. "Of course you wouldn't know, Dear. Though his standing with the *ton* is not on the best terms at the moment, he is after all still the Earl of Kenswick."

Christina exchanged a look with Jane, who mouthed the words "So sorry." She smiled at her friend and looked back at Mrs. Phillips. "On that you are correct, Madam." She held up the package she carried. "Now, if you'll excuse us, we must get this book to my father."

"Yes, and we must find out how long the duke will be in residence at Kenswick so we might issue an invitation to join us for a small dinner party." She smiled fondly at her daughter. "There is so little society here in Malbury and certainly no peers from whom Jane can choose a husband."

Embarrassment lit Jane's face as she said a quick good-bye and hurried her mother on into town.

Christina immediately turned to Helen. "The poor earl! He has no idea the Duke of Northingshire is coming to visit!"

"Never mind that," Helen interjected. "I still cannot get over the fact the duke is here in our little town. Oh, Christina, I have heard he is the most handsome man in all of England! Everyone has been speculating all year that he'll choose a bride soon."

"Helen! We have a much bigger problem!" Christina said. She didn't know of the duke's relationship with Lord Thornton, but if it were a bad one, she didn't want his visit to undo everything she had managed to accomplish.

Helen's eyes lit up. "Perhaps we should go to Kenswick Hall now. Oh, Christina, to think of being in the same room with such an exciting man just makes my heart all aflutter," she gushed, clutching her hands to her heart.

Christina laughed. "Come, come, Helen. We are talking about a duke who probably thinks too much of himself and wouldn't even notice us if we stood right in front of him. All noblemen are very much alike in that respect."

"Lord Thornton has surely noticed you, Christina. I will admit he was a little scary at first, but he has proven to be quite the amusing gentleman in the last week."

Christina relented. "Well, perhaps not all of them are stuffed shirts," she said with a giggle. "But nearly all the rest are!"

Helen sighed. "And perhaps the Duke of Northingshire is one of the exceptions to the rule as Lord Thornton is."

It would seem there would be no talking her out of it. Helen was bound and determined to admire the duke, just as she had been bound and determined to like Nicholas Thornton, the Earl of Kenswick. Perhaps a little visit to the hall to make sure all was right would have a double benefit—she could find out if the duke's visit had upset Lord Thornton, and Helen could see for herself what kind of man the duke was, thus curing all attractions.

"Why don't we stop by Kenswick Hall and find out for ourselves," she told her friend, making up her mind it was the right thing to do.

Helen squealed with delight. "Oh, I am so excited I feel I might burst with happiness!"

"Just make sure you do your bursting *after* we depart, Helen. I would not have you embarrass yourself in front of the duke," Christina teased.

੪

"The Duke of Northingshire is here to see you, my lord," Pierce announced from the study doorway. So rattled by the news was Nicholas that he unconsciously crumpled the paper he'd been making sketches on for his next carving.

When he didn't answer, Pierce cleared his throat and offered, "Would you like me to make excuses, my lord?"

"No!" Nicholas burst out without thinking. But as he said it, he knew that he meant it. North, as he called him, had been his best friend since their days at Eton. Months ago, in his bitterness, he shunned his friend's offer to help and in doing so thought he'd severed their bond.

Could this mean North had forgiven him?

"Send him in here, Pierce." And then as an afterthought, "Please have a pot of tea brought in also."

Pierce bowed. "Very good, Sir."

A minute later, Trevor Kent, the Duke of Northingshire, stepped into the room. North had such a commanding presence about him that even when he walked into a crowded room, a hush would fall and all eyes would turn to him. He was quite a favorite with the ladies, Nicholas knew. With his light blond hair and strong features, he'd heard him likened to Michelangelo's *David*.

Nicholas, however, knew him to be the faithful friend he'd turned his back on when he'd only been trying to help. They'd always been honest with one another, but when North had advised him against breaking his engagement and to curb his wild ways, Nicholas had blown up at him. He told North to stay out of his business and his life, that he didn't need his friendship any longer.

What a fool he'd been. He was so eaten up with self-hatred and bitterness, he'd allowed himself to lose his best friend.

Nicholas stood slowly. Swallowing nervously, not knowing what to say, he finally spoke formally. "It is good to see you, Your Grace."

North grinned. "Well, I must say you are looking better than I imagined. From the accounts of my servants, you've been moping around this empty monstrosity of a house feeling quite sorry for yourself." He drew his gaze to Nicholas's well-cut coat and neatly tied cravat. "I rather expected to see you dressed in sack cloth and ashes, instead of a suit of fine clothes."

All the tension drained out of Nicholas as he smiled and came around his desk to greet his friend. "If you had come a month ago, that is exactly what you would have found." The men clasped hands in a firm, hearty shake. "But I am glad you have come, old friend. I was afraid I had lost your friendship forever."

With his other hand, North gripped his shoulder. "I'll admit to being a little angry at you but when I had time to think on all you'd been through, I knew you just needed time." He stepped back and looked down at Nicholas's leg. "How's that wound healing, by the way? I'm amazed that you walk with barely a limp, considering the doctors had wanted to cut it off!"

Nicholas smoothed a hand down his thigh where the war wound still gave him trouble. "It is better at some times than others," he explained. "But like all the unpleasant events that have happened to me over the last year and a half, I'm learning to live with it."

Moving to the side, he gestured to a couple of chairs in the room. "Please, have a seat. Our tea should arrive in a moment."

North lifted a brow. "Tea? I must say, it's good to see you are not still drinking yourself silly."

Nicholas grimaced. "I gave that up months ago when I

moved into Kenswick. Even in my bitter state, I could see that drinking was only making it worse. So I had decided to shut myself away from the world and wallow in my guilt and grief until. . ." He let his voice drift off.

But North wasn't about to let it go. "Until. . .?"

"Well, until my nephew was given to my care."

"Ah!" North sat back in the cushioned chair, folding his arms on his chest. "So the Wild Rogue of London has finally been tamed by domesticity! I would have thought you'd have shipped the little fellow off to a relative or something. Certainly not try to raise him yourself."

"Well, that is exactly what I wanted to do, except my only living relative, Aunt Wilhelmina, is abroad at the moment. I had no choice but to hire a nan—" He stopped when he saw the grin that creased the big man's face. "Of course. I should have known you had something to do with it."

"Mrs. Sanborne was the nanny for my elder sister's children until they were old enough for a governess and tutor," he explained with a shrug. "I had asked several people about Malbury to keep me informed if you needed anything. When I heard a Miss Wakelin was scouring the shire looking for a nanny, I immediately sent Mrs. Sanborne to her."

Nicholas shook his head in amazement. "You mean you've been looking out for me, even after all I said to you?"

North sat up in his chair, his light blue eyes very serious. "You are my friend, Nicholas. Nothing, not even a few ill-spoken words, will change that."

Swallowing the lump in his throat, Nicholas could only stammer, "I. . .thank you."

North sat back again, his eyes twinkling with mischief. "It's been awhile, old friend, but I can still read you like a book. When you stumbled on your words earlier, you were not going to say your nephew, were you?" He shook a finger at him. "If I didn't know better, I'd say you were about to mention a woman's name."

"And you are grasping for straws!"

"Oh, no." North studied his friend's face thoroughly, giving Nicholas the feeling he could read his mind. "There is something about you that's different, and it could only be two things—either religion or a woman."

Nicholas threw back his head and laughed, just as a maid entered with the tea and proceeded to pour them a cup. He waited until she left the room before he responded. "In my case, those two things go hand in hand." When North gave him a questioning look, he took a sip of his hot tea and said, "She's the vicar's daughter."

ten

"The what?" he sputtered. Nicholas thought for a moment North was going to choke on his tea.

Suddenly, the earl was no longer hesitant of telling his friend about Christina. He needed to talk to somebody about it. "Miss Wakelin, the lady to whom you sent Mrs. Sanborne, is the true reason I have begun living life once again."

North patted his mouth with his napkin. "Nicholas, there was a time when you would not even look a young lady's way unless she was no less than the daughter of a viscount!" He paused a moment, as if measuring his next words. "That is the main reason you became engaged to Katherine."

Nicholas nodded. "I know, but I think differently now. *She* has changed me." He stood and started pacing about the room as he searched for the words to explain. "She is different from any woman I have ever known. She is funny and kind, yet determined. She doesn't simper and talk about silly things like so many other ladies, and she speaks without guile, in a straightforward manner that I find refreshing." He threw up his hands. "She has won over the whole staff here at Kenswick Hall, practically has them eating out of her hand, yet she isn't manipulative, she's just. . .herself," he said, unable to find the appropriate words.

"This is unbelievable," North said, and Nicholas whirled around ready to do battle over those words. But when he saw the look of amused yet puzzled incredulity on his friend's face, he came over and sat back down.

"Why is it so hard to believe?" he asked calmly as he picked up his cup again.

"You are in love with her!"

Nicholas balked at the use of the "L" word. "I never said that."

North shook his head. "You didn't have to. It was in your face, your words, as you spoke of her." He paused for a moment, his gaze intently on Nicholas. "Love is so rare, Nick, that when you find it, you have to acknowledge it."

Nicholas let North's words penetrate his heart. Did he love Christina? He was certainly fond of her, so much so he seemed to crave her company all the time. But still, with all that had happened to him, he needed to sort through his feelings before he could make such an acknowledgment to himself.

"I know you are right. I just don't want to make any more mistakes," he said after a moment.

An understanding smile curved North's lips. "Indeed, I do understand." He set down his cup and smacked the armrests with his palms. "Now when do I get to meet this paragon?"

Nicholas smiled, stood up, and walked to the window. Peering out to the garden, he motioned for North to join him. "I thought she might be here. There she is."

North joined Nicholas in looking out to where Christina and Helen stood with Mrs. Sanborne. Ty was in Christina's arms, and she was smiling down at him as she lightly swung him back and forth.

"She's lovely," North whispered almost reverently as his

gaze took in the sight before him. "Look at all that glorious red hair. What a splash she'd make amongst the *ton.*"

Nicholas shuddered at the thought. "And subject her innocence to the immoral behavior of the upper classes? Never." He stared at her a moment more before looking over at North. "We are from two different worlds, North. I'm not sure either of us would fit into the other's world, even if she wanted to."

"You can do almost anything if you want something badly enough."

"But at what expense?" Nicholas murmured more to himself than to his friend.

"I want to meet her!" North declared as he turned from the window and started across the study. When he got to the door, he looked imperially at Nicholas. "Well? Are you coming or not?"

Nicholas laughed. "Only if you'll remember I saw her first. Absolutely no flirting!"

North shrugged in an arrogant manner. "Women have always seemed to like me, Nick. There's never been a need to flirt."

"I'm surprised they could fit in the same room with you with such an inflated ego filling the space!" Nicholas retorted as he slapped him on the shoulders and led the way to the garden.

❧

"Oh, dear. Oh, dear! They're coming, Christina, they're coming!" Helen smoothed her light blue dress and patted her fat curls. "How do I look? Am I presentable?"

Christina looked at her beautiful friend and knew Helen was much more presentable than she. Already her hair had come loose from the topknot she'd pinned it into this morning, and now it was flying wildly about her face and past her shoulders. Ty had spit up on her dress, and it was wrinkled from holding him.

In short, she was embarrassed at being introduced to a duke looking as she did, but there was nothing for it.

Throwing her misgivings to the wind, she smiled and waved to the men as they came near.

"My lord! You're just in time for our daily walk through the garden," she called out as she placed Ty into his pram.

"Excellent," he called back in reply. After a few moments, they had reached the women.

"Miss Wakelin, Miss Nichols, may I present an old friend of mine, Trevor Kent, the Duke of Northingshire. Mrs. Sanborne, I believe you are already acquainted?"

"Your grace," the women said in unison as they curtsied.

"It is a stupendous pleasure to see you once again, your grace," Mrs. Sanborne added. "Stupendous!"

Christina noticed the handsome duke took great care not to smile as he nodded her direction. "Indeed, it is my pleasure, Mrs. Sanborne, that you were able to help Lord Thornton with his nephew."

A few other pleasantries were said before the nanny took control of the pram and went ahead of them on the path.

Nicholas held out his arm to Christina. "Shall we?"

Christina told herself her heart should not be racing madly just because he asked to walk with her. But it did no good. With her heart pounding, she took his arm.

Beside them she noticed the Duke of Northingshire, or North, as he asked them to call him, had offered the same to Helen.

For one horrific moment, Helen became so pale Christina thought she might faint dead away, right there on the garden path. But her fanciful friend recovered, and a big smile curved her lips as she slipped her hand through the duke's arm.

They had walked a short distance when North remarked, "I have heard it is you I should thank, Miss Wakelin, for this remarkable turnaround in my friend here. I had despaired that he might be lost to us forever."

Christina glanced surprisingly up at Lord Thornton. Her heart tripped a beat when he smiled down at her. Swallowing hard, she pulled her eyes away from his and looked at the duke. "I would not say that, your grace. It is God who led me to his lordship. I just knew I had to let him know he is much too important to God and his friends to shut himself away from everyone."

North smiled but looked puzzled. "If Nick had shut himself away from everyone, how did you meet?"

Wincing a little with embarrassment, Christina opened her mouth to explain, but the earl interjected. "She climbed my tree, then fell out of it and straight into my arms. My life has not been the same since."

Christina stared at Lord Thornton with amazement. He made the whole encounter seem so. . .*romantic!*

"Surely you jest! I cannot imagine this proper young woman climbing a tree!" North laughed.

"Oh, she climbed it all right. I was there every horrifying moment of it!" Helen exclaimed. "I tried to talk her out of it, but when Christina gets something in her mind, there is no stopping her."

North laughed again. "A woman with determination! I like that."

Helen quickly changed her tune. "Of course, I would have climbed the tree with her, but I thought someone needed to stand by as a lookout in case the earl came by."

Christina smothered a giggle at Helen's obvious tactics.

"You know, Helen, I didn't know you had been there with Christina. I saw no one until I heard the cry of my poor cat up in the tree."

"When she spotted you coming near us, I told her to leave so that she would not get into trouble also," Christina explained. "She argued, but I insisted!"

They had almost circled the perimeter of the garden when Lord Thornton bent down to her ear. "I have something I would like to give you."

His breath at her ear warmed her as she turned to look at him. So close was he that she could see tiny gold flecks in his eyes that she had never noticed before. Staring into those eyes made her feel strange yet wonderful at the same time.

"What is it?" she asked, loving the fact he still had not pulled back from her.

His intense gaze swept her face like a loving caress. "If you can try to get away from the others in an hour from now, I will meet you under the gazebo just on the outskirts of the garden, over there." He nodded toward the ornate white structure standing a few yards from them.

She wanted to say yes, but it did not seem proper. "I don't think. . ."

Nicholas cut her off. "I promise it will only be for a few moments. I have nothing improper in mind. Your reputation will remain safe."

Her heart won out over her head. "All right," she answered.

He covered her hand with his free hand before letting her go. "It's been a pleasure to walk with you this afternoon, ladies. I hate to end our time together, but I must see that North is settled into a suite."

Helen reluctantly let go of North's arm after Christina gave her a pointed look.

"How long will you be at Kenswick Hall, your grace?" Helen blurted out.

North seemed unruffled by her too-eager tone. "Only for a few days, I'm afraid. I have business to take care of at my estate near Edinburgh."

When Christina thought her friend might burst into tears at that news, she quickly stepped in front of her to cut off the duke's view. "Well, it's been nice making your acquaintance, your grace. I'm sure we'll see you on the morrow."

From the twinkle in the large man's eyes, Christina knew she hadn't fooled him. "Indeed, I shall look forward to it. Good afternoon."

After an hour had passed, Christina convinced Helen to check on the puppies in the stables so she could run over to the gazebo.

Lord Thornton was already there, standing so tall and handsome as the rays of the sinking sun shone through the latticework and touched his manly features. Taking a deep breath, she stepped into the gazebo, not daring to come too close to him.

Neither of them spoke. Words didn't seem to be required as they stood staring into each other's eyes.

Slowly he brought his hand from behind his back, and within it he held an exquisite glass case about six inches tall. She took the case and brought it closer to peer inside.

And what she saw took her breath away—a carved figurine of a woman holding a puppy in her arms.

The woman was Christina. Every detail of her face, hair, and dress was so true to life.

"Do you like it?" Nicholas asked.

Looking up at him, she could tell he was nervous about giving it to her, unsure of how she would feel.

Without thinking about it, Christina reached up and kissed him on his rough cheek. "It so beautiful, my lord. I cannot express what it means to me that you have made this for me."

Nicholas took her arms in a soft, caressing grip. Emotions she couldn't understand flashed over his handsome face, and she wondered if he might kiss her.

Oh, she hoped he would. She wished he would take her into his strong arms and tell her he was falling in love with her, just as she was falling for him.

Suddenly he let his hands drop and stepped back from her. Confused, Christina looked searchingly at him, but it was impossible to read his thoughts, for his face was turned away.

"Perhaps you should go before Helen wonders where you are," he told her, his voice gravelly.

Christina wanted to cry. She must have done something wrong. Of course! He must have thought it untoward for her to kiss him like that. Sickened that she'd shamed herself, she mumbled, "Yes, I should go." Clutching the glass case protectively to her, she ran from the gazebo.

☙

Nicholas banged his hand on the post of the gazebo in frustration and anger. He'd promised not only Christina but also her father that he would not act improperly.

But there he was, all set to take her into his arms and kiss her.

Filled with self-loathing and disgust, he railed at himself for bringing her out to the garden alone. He should have just wrapped the gift up as a parcel and had it delivered to her house.

But he'd been so excited about seeing her face when she realized the figurine was of her. He'd even gone into town just to purchase the case, causing a lot of gossip and speculation in the process, he was sure.

He should have done better. He should not have compromised her honor by getting her alone.

She deserved a gentleman who did not make such foolish mistakes. She deserved someone who did not have an ugly past. She deserved a man of impeccable reputation.

In short, she did not deserve him.

Yet, she had faith in him.

Christina told him God also believed in him and could help him.

So for the first time since he was a young boy, Nicholas Thornton, the sixth Earl of Kenswick, the most notorious rake in all of England, kneeled down on the whitewashed boards of the gazebo. . .and prayed.

eleven

The next morning was bright and sunny. Almost everyone in Malbury seemed to be outdoors, walking their dogs, playing with their children, or just strolling about for exercise.

It was a day that should have brightened everyone's mood. But as Christina stared glumly out her window, she could not drum up so much as a smile, her spirits were so low.

She'd already made the decision to stay home today and not go on her daily visit to Kenswick Hall. How could she face him after behaving so boldly? What must he think of her?

She took her eyes from the window and looked down at the figurine in her hand. As her fingers caressed the smoothly carved wood, she marveled again at how much care had gone into the figurine.

Why did he make it? Did she mean something to him? Did he think of her as a cousin or friend?

With a sigh of frustration, she went over to her nightstand and put the figurine back into its glass container. Spending all her time having romantic thoughts about the Earl of Kenswick was not doing her any good.

"Miss Christina!" Mrs. Hopkins called through her door, knocking gently. Glad to have a diversion from her troubles, she called for the housekeeper to come in.

Excitement flushed her plump cheeks and her hands fluttered around nervously. "Oh, Miss! I've never seen the like. Gentlemen such as these, and here in your father's cottage!"

Christina went quickly to her. "Take a calming breath, Mrs. Hopkins. I'm afraid I do not follow. What gentlemen are here?"

"Lord Thornton and another gentleman. A tall man with fancy clothes and almost as handsome as the earl himself. They are something to behold, I'm telling you, Miss. Quite takes the breath clear out of me!"

Christina was having trouble breathing herself at the news. "Lord Thornton? Here?" When Mrs. Hopkins nodded, Christina let go of her hands and whirled to face her large oval mirror. "He must have the Duke of Northinghsire with him!"

"A duke, did you say?" the housekeeper gasped. "Oh, dear, and with no warning too! I still haven't done the dusting!"

Christina tried to tidy her hair, but the curls kept springing out everywhere. Giving up, she grabbed a ribbon and tied it back in a ponytail. "It's all right, Mrs. Hopkins. I'm sure they won't notice," she said, though her thoughts were on other things than the dusting.

What did he want? Was he here to see her?

"Mrs. Hopkins, I believe there's someone at the door!" her father's voice called from downstairs, startling both women.

"Oh, dear, oh, my! I hope I can remember the proper etiquette for handling one of the *ton!*" the elder woman fretted as she scurried to the door.

Christina turned back to the mirror and wished, as she had a thousand times before, that she was more sophisticated in appearance, more dainty and elegant. Her gown was a recent style, but with her height and lack of grace, she would never be mistaken for a peer.

Wishing, however, would get her nowhere. She was who she was and no amount of wishing would make her something she was not. And, besides, she'd always liked who she was. Why should she suddenly want to change everything about herself just because she'd become acquainted with a nobleman?

Maybe because you want him to like you, a voice whispered in her head.

Angry with herself for having such vain thoughts, she turned away from the mirror and waited by her door to see if the earl had, indeed, come to see her.

☙

"Tell me again why we have come to the vicar's house," North whispered to Nicholas as they sat in the parlor where the housekeeper had sent them. It had been quite an amusing welcome, as the woman greeted them both with such a deep curtsy, the men thought they were going to have to help her up.

"Because I want to ask Reverend Wakelin's permission to see his daughter today."

"Hmm," North grunted with a puzzled frown. "And why could you not just wait until she came to Kenswick Hall? Doesn't she visit your nephew every day?"

"Because I felt I needed to make an apology to both Miss Wakelin and her father for my bad behavior yesterday," he explained evenly while keeping an eye on the door, waiting for the vicar to come into the room.

"I'm sorry, but I don't follow," his friend replied.

Nicholas let out a nervous breath. "I asked Miss Wakelin to meet me in the gazebo alone so I might give her a gift." He ran a hand through his hair. "I almost kissed her!" he blurted out in a harsh whisper.

North stared at him as if he were speaking a language he

could not understand. "I beg your pardon. You *almost* kissed her? That's what this whole thing is about?"

"Yes."

"Did she protest?"

"No."

"Slap you?"

"Of course not."

"Call you a cad and a rake?"

"Don't be ridiculous."

North scratched his head. "Did she act as though she wanted to kiss you, then?"

"I thought she did, because she kissed me on my cheek, and it compelled it to take her arms and bring her closer. But she was only thanking me for the gift I gave her. I realized in the nick of time."

"Sooo, let me understand this," North stated slowly. "You are upset because Miss Wakelin kissed you, and you thought it an invitation to take it a step further and kiss her back. Do I have that right?"

Nicholas threw up his hands. "Yes, except I had promised her father I would stay away from her. Instead, I encouraged her to meet me without her chaperone and all but embraced her! I also promised her that if she'd meet me, I would do nothing improper."

North shook his head. "Really, Man, you're being too hard on yourself. What is a kiss after all? I daresay it wouldn't be the first lips you've kissed."

"You are thinking about London society, where flirtations are a way of life. This is the country, where even a kiss could cause a scandal."

North was about to comment when they heard the door

to the parlor open, and in walked the Reverend Wakelin. "Well, Lord Thornton, so good to see you again. And I see you've brought a friend."

Nicholas made a quick introduction of North and got right to the matter at hand. "Reverend, I came today because—"

"Because you have decided to join us tomorrow for Sunday service! How lovely of you to come by and let us know," Christina said as she breezed through the doorway, putting herself between the vicar and Nicholas.

Nicholas stared at her with surprise, not understanding the warning look she flashed him with her bright eyes. "Uh. . .I'm not sure. . . ," he stammered.

Christina was mouthing something, but he couldn't quite make it out.

She turned to North with a big smile and said, "And you, Lord Kent, will you be joining us also?"

Nicholas should have known North would find the whole conversation amusing. His friend smiled back at her. "I wouldn't miss it for the world, Miss Wakelin."

"Excellent!" she cried as she whirled around to face her father.

"If you don't mind, Papa, I will walk with the gentlemen back to Kenswick Hall. I need to check on little Ty as well as feed the pups Lord Thornton has been boarding for me in his stables."

Nicholas watched as her father gave her a shrewd look that told everyone he wasn't fooled by her act for a moment. His eyes swept past his daughter to give Nicholas a questioning stare.

"We would be happy to escort your daughter, Sir," Nicholas told him.

The vicar nodded but glanced back at Christina. "I don't know what you are up to, Daughter, but be assured I will find out." He sighed and patted her on the cheek. "And please try to be on your best behavior. I would have Lord Thornton believe you have matured since the time you were a little girl and pushed his female friend into the lake!"

"Papa!" Christina gasped with embarrassment, as both Nicholas and the duke burst out in laughter.

"Good day, my lord, your grace," he told them both with a nod before he exited the room.

On the walk to Kenswick Hall, Nicholas stopped her and demanded, "Can you tell me what that was all about?"

Christina looked up at him. "I heard you!"

"You heard what?"

"I heard you two talking about what you were planning to do! My room is directly above the parlor and the sound carries." She shook her head. "I can't believe you were going to tell my father about our meeting in the gazebo and about the kiss I gave you!"

"Miss Wakelin, I was just going to apologize for my own bad behavior," Nicholas tried to explain.

"I was the one who kissed you, my lord. I could not sleep all night for wondering what you must think of me."

Nicholas couldn't believe what he was hearing. "Miss Wakelin, you are not to blame, and I was flattered by your kiss. It's just that I promised your father I would not be alone with you. I felt ashamed that I'd gone back on my promise and then almost kissed you."

Christina frowned. "There, you see, it is all my fault. My kiss caused you to get carried away on the wings of romantic emotions."

Nicholas stared at her blankly. "On the wings of what?"

She sighed with forbearance as if she were dealing with a child. "On the wings of romantic emotion. Helen told me that in her gothic romance books, this often happens to men when a woman gets too close."

A loud blast of laughter startled them both. They turned to see North shaking his head as he tried to curb his mirth. "I'm sorry, but you two are more entertaining than the comedy I saw last month in a London theatre."

Christina covered her mouth in horror. "Oh, dear. I forgot you were there, your grace."

This time it was Nicholas who laughed, especially at the bemused expression on North's face. "I daresay he hasn't heard that many times in his life."

North grinned. "Indeed. I believe I've changed my mind about going back to the hall and favor a walk in the country instead. Miss Wakelin, would you please excuse me if I cannot help Nick escort you the rest of the way?"

She smiled back at him. "Of course."

North had the audacity to wink at them both before walking away. Subtlety was not one of his virtues.

Taking Christina by the arm, Nicholas turned her toward him. "Miss Wakelin, before we come to Kenswick, I want to be sure everything is all right between us—that you are not upset at me."

Her smile was so breathtaking, he wished he could kiss her. Perhaps Helen's books were not too far from the truth where "romantic emotions" were concerned. But a kiss was not the most important thing he desired. No, he wanted to put his arms around her and just hold her—to claim to the world that she was his.

He wanted her to return those romantic feelings.

She liked him, he could tell. But he could not tell if that liking ended at friendship or not. Perhaps she was after her first objective where he was concerned, to help him find God again.

If he told her he had begun to pray again, would she feel her duty was done and stop coming to his home?

He wasn't going to take that chance. Not yet.

"Of course I am not upset! The figurine you made me was the most beautiful gift anyone has ever given me. I shall treasure it always. But you must forgive me for being so bold, my lord. I reacted before I thought about it."

Her words filled him with hope. "If you were not so bold, you would not be the Christina Wakelin I have come to know since childhood. You are the most unique woman I have ever met, and you constantly keep me on my toes!"

"I can't tell if that was a complaint or a compliment," Christina said.

He laughed. "Most definitely a compliment."

Nicholas held out his arm. "Now that we've cleared the air, shall we continue on to Kenswick Hall?"

She placed her hand in the crook of his arm, and it felt so right to be by his side—like she truly belonged there.

As they walked, Nicholas dared to ask one more thing. "Do you suppose now that we've become such good friends, you can call me Nicholas?"

"Thank you!" she cried out with relief. "We have so few neighbors with titles that it has been hard to remember to refer to you as 'my lord.'"

"I've been acknowledged by some sort of title or other since birth. I suppose I don't even notice it."

"I think it would be very hard to get used to, all that bowing and scraping people do just because of some exalted title you had nothing to do with!"

An enigmatic smile crept over his face. "I think you could get used to almost anything, Christina. Even an exalted title."

She shrugged. "There's no point in arguing, since I shall never be in such a position anyway."

Never say never, dear Christina, Nicholas thought to himself, determination strengthening his resolve to be the kind of man she could love.

Never say never.

twelve

"I'm in love, I just know it. I've got this nervous feeling in my chest and I feel quite dizzy when I look at him, so it must be love."

"Either that or you're coming down with a bad cold," Christina said to Helen in a wry voice. She really wished the duke would leave Kenswick so her friend would cease making a fool of herself over the man.

"No, no. I'm quite sure of my feeling," Helen continued with firm resolve. "We shall have a large wedding, since he is quite known in England, and a long wedding trip to Paris, Rome, and possibly Milan."

Christina rolled her eyes in exasperation. "Dear Helen, it is good to dream big dreams, as long as you can separate fancy from truth." She gave her friend a gentle look. "You know as well as I the Duke of Northingshire must marry within his social class. It would never be accepted by his family if he decided to marry a commoner."

Helen sighed. "Yes, but miracles have been known to happen. Just look at you and Lord Thornton."

Christina frowned. "For the last time, Helen, Nicholas and I are just friends. Anything more is impossible!"

Helen leveled a gaze at Christina. "I know when a man's smitten with a woman, and Nicholas Thornton is that man! Lord Kent does not yet display his feelings when he looks at me, but given a little time I'm sure he'll come around."

Poor North had been wearing more the look of a hunted man these last three days. More often than not, when he walked into a room and saw Helen there, he quickly walked right back out.

Christina had tried to warn Helen that ladies do not pursue gentlemen so blatantly, but she merely replied that she was going to be twenty-two in a month and was not getting any younger.

Christina could have told Helen that Archie McGregor, a young Scott who'd just inherited a farm in Malbury, had tried in vain to speak with her several times in church lately. But Christina doubted Helen would even hear her.

Soon North would leave and Helen would be able to come to her senses again.

Christina stood up from the bench they were sitting on, located within the church courtyard, and tightened the ties to her bonnet. It was Sunday, and the two had been enjoying the sunlight while they waited for the service to start.

"Well, I suppose we must go inside," she told Helen with a sigh. She tried to sound more cheerful, but it was difficult.

Nicholas had not come.

Knowing her thoughts, Helen stood and linked her arm with Christina's. "I'm sure he's just delayed."

Christina nodded. "I'm sure you're right. Yet I can't help feeling I bullied him into this."

"Well, come along. Waiting out here is just making you worry."

The choir had begun to sing the first few measures of a hymn when a low hum of whispers started at the back and quickly filtered its way forward in the church. The more indiscreet of the parishioners craned their necks to see who had come through the door, while others made a subtle show of taking peeks behind their fans.

Christina, however, had no need to look back for she knew exactly who it was.

The Earl of Kenswick had come to church.

From her pew, Christina had an excellent view of the two gentlemen, but her eyes studied only one of them. He was so handsome in his black coat and gray britches. He'd even trimmed his hair. He looked every bit the nobleman he was, and it was a heavy reminder that his station was so far above her own. All her feelings for him were going to cause her nothing but pain. They were from two completely different worlds.

Why couldn't she remember that?

"Oh, here they come!" Helen whispered excitedly as they stood outside the church after the service ended.

All the love she felt in her heart came bubbling to the forefront the moment she too spotted the men coming their direction.

Nicholas gave Christina a teasing grin. "Were you worried I wouldn't show?"

She suppressed a smile and gave him a mock glare. "Were you late just to make me worried?"

North threw back his head with a booming laugh that drew everyone's attention. "I really like this girl, Nick," he declared as he slapped his friend on the back. Then to Christina he said, "It's too bad you were never presented at court. With your wit and spunk, you'd be declared an original!"

Nicholas shook his head, laughing. "It would never work. In town there are too few trees to climb and animals to doctor. Christina would be like a fish out of water."

"Well, ladies, we'll bid you a good day," he told them after his laughter subsided. "But before we go, I would like to invite you to tea, along with Mrs. Sanborne and Ty, of course, this afternoon."

Annoyed that he thought her so unsophisticated, it was on the tip of Christina's tongue to refuse when Helen broke in with, "We'll be there!"

"Splendid!" Nicholas declared, while giving Christina a curious look.

After the men walked away, Christina noticed that almost the entire congregation was still standing in the church courtyard, staring at her with speculation.

Straightening her backbone, she forced herself to smile and mingle among the crowd, speaking pointedly to each one, inquiring about children and health and anything her mind could think of. If she pretended all was normal, then perhaps they'd believe it.

But everything wasn't normal. She was in love with a man who was far beyond her reach. That fact was made even more clear that afternoon when she and Helen went for tea at Kenswick Hall.

❧

Christina held Ty on her lap, and Mrs. Sanborne was making everyone laugh with a story of how the baby had rolled off his mat and under the decorative skirt of his baby bed. She'd ransacked the room in a panic before he came rolling right back out.

Christina was looking down at the baby with a smile when the laughter came to a strange, abrupt halt. She looked up to find out the reason for the sudden silence and noticed every eye was turned toward the parlor door.

"Well, Nephew, have you lost all your manners, or will you give your aunt a proper greeting?"

Christina's eyes flew to the door, where she found a short, trim woman, her nose and chin thrust upward. As her cold blue eyes scanned the room, they soon came to rest on Christina.

A look of horror crossed her aging features as she fastened her dagger gaze back on Nicholas.

Nicholas, as well as North, had stood up the moment she spoke, and both men bowed in her direction. "Aunt Willie. So good of you to visit. I had heard you were abroad," Nicholas greeted smoothly, his face unreadable.

His aunt's chin rose even higher as she frowned and made a sniffing noise. "Do not call me that atrocious name! Now, I would like to know if the baby being held by that unfamiliar young woman over there is my great nephew."

Nicholas glanced at Christina and then turned back to his aunt. "Yes, it is. Now let me make introductions," he began as he motioned toward the duke first. "You know North, of course."

"Of course," she answered with an imperial nod. "I've known his grace's family for many years."

"Always a pleasure, my lady," North greeted with another bow.

He motioned to Mrs. Sanborne. "This is my nephew's nanny, Mrs. Sanborne." He turned to his employee. "Mrs. Sanborne, this is my aunt, Lady Wilhelmina Stanhope."

Christina watched as the nanny rose to greet the lady but was cut short when the haughty woman didn't even acknowledge her presence. Instead she glared at Christina and Helen.

"And who are they?" she demanded.

"These dear ladies have been a great help to me since my nephew came to Kenswick. May I present Miss Christina Wakelin and Miss Helen Nichols," Nicholas replied, his voice filled with warmth as he spoke.

Lady Wilhelmina's sharp gaze focused on Christina. "Wakelin? Where do I know that name from? Who is her father?"

Christina answered before Nicholas could. "My father is Reverend Wakelin, the vicar of Malbury."

"I see," the woman said, her tone suggesting the information was of no importance. "Well, it appears I have come none too soon. Nicholas, have my rooms readied. I shall need to rest before I rectify this dreadful situation you have gotten yourself into. And do not doubt that I have heard of your abhorrent behavior in London and your withdrawal from society. That is another matter that needs my immediate attention. Now ring your man and let's get on with it!"

Christina glanced at Nicholas and noticed the muscle in his jaw clenched with tension. "Pierce!" he bellowed. The butler appeared right away.

"Yes, my lord?"

"Have the upstairs maids prepare my aunt's rooms right away."

Pierce bowed. "Very good, my lord." He bowed to Lady Stanhope. "My lady? This way, if you please."

Without a second glance at anyone, she marched out of the room behind Pierce.

For a moment no one spoke. "What do you think she meant by rectifying a dreadful situation?" North finally asked.

Nicholas shook his head while raking a hand through his curls. "I was afraid to ask."

Christina had the feeling the "dreadful situation" had something to do with her. Standing up, she carried Ty over to Mrs. Sanborne. "I think it best we leave," she said, looking toward the earl.

North nodded. "I believe my time here has come to an end also. I need to get up to my estate in Scotland."

"What you both are saying is that you are abandoning me, am I right?"

Christina grinned as she and North exchanged a glance. "Yes," they replied together.

"But. . .but you cannot leave!" Helen cried as she stood up and looked wildly in North's direction.

"Now, now, Helen," Christina said. "I realize we'll both miss our newly acquired friend, but I'm sure he'll visit Kenswick Hall again." She maintained a death grip on her friend's arm.

"'Tis so!" North concurred. "But it shall not be until the new year. I will be journeying to America from Scotland and will not be back for some months."

Helen started to protest, but Christina whispered in her ear, "Perhaps distance will make his heart grow fonder!" She felt guilty for giving Helen false hope, but at least it worked, for her friend stifled whatever she was going to say.

Nicholas grimaced. "So I will have to deal with my new visitor alone, I see."

"She is, after all, your aunt," Christina teased. "Surely she can't be all that terrifying."

"You'd be surprised," Nicholas replied.

thirteen

It didn't take long for Nicholas to realize his aunt's sole purpose for being at Kenswick Hall. She intended to ruin his life.

Or so it seemed.

"Now, I have already sent out invitations." She stopped and glared at her nephew. "Nicholas, do pay attention, Dear. I'm doing all this for your benefit!"

From behind his desk, Nicholas stifled a sigh and drew his tired gaze to the settee his aunt was perched on. "Aunt Willie, I know you mean well, but I do not feel like entertaining members of the *ton* here at Kenswick. If I can refresh your memory, I'm not exactly in the *ton*'s favor at the moment, and I've grown quite provincial in the last few months. I relish the peace and quiet the country provides. If you bring strangers here, it will no longer be so."

"It's Aunt Wilhelmina, and these are not strangers we are talking about. These are your peers. Peers that are all set to forgive your lapse in decorum, especially since I explained the reason you behaved that way."

Nicholas found it hard to clamp down his anger. His life was finally getting to the point where he enjoyed it again. He liked the person he was becoming, and he enjoyed being with the lady who had helped him get there.

His aunt's interference in his life could ruin everything.

"Let's be honest, shall we, Aunt? Every family that is on

126

your list has a daughter of marital age. It is your plan, is it not? To get me married?"

She seemed unconcerned that he was upset. With a shrug of her shoulders, she told him, "Yes, I will not deny it. You have a child to raise, and every child deserves a mother." She held out her hand to examine one of the diamond rings on her fingers. "And I would not have enlisted the help of the local riff-raff to help with the baby. Really, Nicholas! The vicar's daughter?"

"For your information, Christina Wakelin helped me at a time when no one else would, and I would not have her spoken of in such uncomplimentary terms!" he said as he stood and glared down at his aunt.

"You seem to be quite fond of this woman, Nicholas, and though she has come to your aid, it is simply not done!" his aunt snapped back, she too rising from her seat.

"She is none of your business," he stated slowly through gritted teeth.

"No, but you are, and I will see that you are taken care of."

"I am thirty years old, Aunt, and long past needing your care!"

She gasped. "You impertinent boy! I will have—"

"Excuse me, my lord," Pierce spoke from the doorway, interrupting the tense exchange.

"Yes, what is it, Pierce?"

"Miss Wakelin has asked to see you in the garden. It concerns the young master."

Without a glance at his aunt, Nicholas sprinted toward the door, ignoring her as she called out his name.

He was out of breath from running by the time he reached the garden. When he saw Christina and Ty, it took him a few seconds to realize they both seemed fine. They were sitting alone in the center of the garden on a blanket, the baby in Christina's arms.

"What is wrong?" he asked.

Christina turned her radiant smile to him. "There is nothing wrong. Ty has just done something remarkable, and I thought you'd like to see it." She lay the baby face down on the blanket. "Now watch this!"

He watched as the wiggly little creature waved his arms and legs about, then braced his arms on either side of him and sat upright.

Christina began to clap and coo all sorts of praise to Ty, who responded by plopping back down on the blanket. She patted his back. "See!" she exclaimed to Nicholas. "Isn't that amazing?"

The only thing Nicholas found amazing was how the sunlight shone on her lovely face. But, of course, he had the sense not to say that.

She, however, was expecting some sort of reaction, so he did the best he could. "Umm, yes, quite amazing," he said.

Christina was not so easily fooled. "You weren't even paying attention," she countered with a frown.

"Of course I was."

Taking the baby in her arms, she patted the space beside them. "Have a seat. Ty, I'm sure, would love to visit with you this morning."

Did she also want to spend time with him, or was it only one-sided? Was he the only one who felt this warmth and kinship between them? Nicholas wasted no time in doing as she asked, and when she placed Ty in his arms, he realized holding the baby was becoming more comfortable.

"You are getting quite good at that, my lord!" Christina said.

Nicholas smiled proudly as he cradled the baby close and kissed him on the forehead. "Yes, I am!" he admitted immodestly, making her laugh.

For a few moments they sat together talking about the baby in contented companionship. *This is what it must feel like to have a family*, Nicholas thought. A sense of completeness, of warmth and love, enveloped them like a cocoon.

And he did love her. With every fiber of his being, he wanted this woman to be his wife and to live with him forever.

But he could not. So much stood between them. Yet, if only he knew that she loved him in return, none of the obstacles would stop him from making her his own.

"Are you enjoying your visit with Lady Stanhope?" Christina asked, breaking through his heavy thoughts.

"Unfortunately, the word *enjoy* is usually absent when dealing with Aunt Willie. She is determined to insert herself into my life and wreak havoc on it."

"Perhaps if you spoke to her and made her understand. . ."

"I've talked until I am weary of it, and yet it will not stop her. My aunt has already invited half the *ton* to Kenswick Hall beginning tomorrow afternoon," he confessed.

Her eyes filled with compassion. "Oh, Nicholas! Does she not know all you've been through in the last few months?"

Nicholas gazed at her with wonderment. This beautiful woman actually cared about his welfare. Wasn't that a beginning to love?

He prayed it was so.

"My aunt knows some of it, at least what gossip has come her way, but she believes this is the best solution for my situation." He took a fortifying breath and gave her a searching look. "She is trying to make a good match for me. These families she has invited all have daughters. She intends that I choose one to marry."

Nicholas saw surprise and dismay fill Christina's eyes. It was a reaction that gave him hope. "Oh," she murmured. She tried to smile at him.

She failed wonderfully.

"Of course, I have no intention of going along with her plan," he said carefully, gauging her reaction.

Her eyes widened. "You don't?"

He shook his head slowly, never taking his gaze off her. "No."

He wished he could read her thoughts, but her expression became shuttered as she looked away. "But I thought you had changed your mind about living a life of solitude."

"Oh, I have. I do not know what I must have been thinking to believe I would be happy without a wife and family." He took a chance and reached out to lift her chin so that she was staring back at him. "And my change of heart is all because of you."

"I hope I have been of some help. But above all I wanted you to realize God still loves you and never gave up on you."

Nicholas smiled as his thumb caressed her jawline. "How could I not know God loves me, Christina? After all, He sent me you, didn't He?"

She visibly swallowed as she looked at him with hope and wariness all at once. Did he dare hope that she understood he had strong feelings for her?

For a moment, her eyes grew luminous with emotion, but then she pulled away from his touch and started fiddling with the baby's toys scattered on the blanket. "I was just doing what I felt God was asking me to do," she said, her eyes refusing to look at him.

"Christina!" he whispered roughly, stopping one of her hands by covering it with his own. "What I'm trying to tell you is that I—"

"Whatever are you doing there on that filthy ground— and holding the baby no less?" Aunt Wilhelmina's voice boomed as she marched over to where they sat. "And where is the nanny? Shouldn't she be looking after the child?"

Nicholas quickly let go of Christina's hand when his aunt appeared, but he knew she had witnessed it. Her eyes were narrowed with suspicion, her nostrils flared with indignation.

"Aunt Willie, will you please give us a moment? There are some things I need to discuss with Christina," Nicholas tried to explain.

"I most certainly will not!" She looked scathingly at Christina. "Young lady, have you no manners or decency? Where is your chaperone? Why have you been left with my grandnephew when you are not trained?"

"My chaperone got a splinter in her hand, and Mrs. Sanborne took her to her room to extract it," Christina said evenly. "I have looked after not only this child, but also many children before. I can assure you I am well capable of dealing with a baby."

He admired the calm way Christina spoke but knew his aunt was going to ruin everything.

"Aunt Wilhelmina, please give me a moment. I shall meet with you directly," he stated again.

"There is no time," she snapped. "Our first guests, the Birkenstocks, have arrived earlier than expected. They are awaiting you in the drawing room."

Nicholas closed his eyes a moment to get hold of his flaring temper. "I cannot believe you are interfering in my life this way!" he said, his voice gritty with aggravation.

"Believe it and accept it." She took a deep breath, causing the sapphires at her throat to glimmer in the sunlight. "Now do come along. Let's hope you have not wrinkled your clothes too badly by frolicking on the ground like a petty commoner."

Beside him, Nicholas saw Christina stiffen at her cruel words. She reached over and took the baby from his arms, her eyes downcast and her expression stony. "I'll take the baby to Mrs. Sanborne," she murmured.

"No!" he bellowed, startling both women and making the baby cry. Turning to his aunt, he lowered his tone. "Tell the Birkenstocks I will see them in a moment, Aunt. There will be no discussions on this point!"

Wisely, his aunt relented, albeit with disdain. She spun about and marched away from them, her displeasure sounding in every step she took.

"I think it best I go in," Christina said.

Nicholas put his hand on her shoulder. "Christina, I apologize for my aunt's behavior. Her opinions are not my own." When he saw that she was not going to flee, he let go of her shoulder. "Now, there is something I would like to ask you before I go in."

"What is it?"

"Well," he hesitated, "I don't quite know how to say this. . . ."

"You don't need me to come here anymore," she surmised wrongly. "It's all right, really. I—"

"Christina!" he interrupted. "Of course I don't want you

to stop coming to Kenswick. In fact, your presence here means a great deal to me, and that's what I need to talk to you about."

She looked at him a little warily. "I don't understand."

"Christina. . .I need to know just. . .how you. . ." He stumbled. Then, taking a deep breath, he blurted out what he needed to say. "I need to know what your feelings are toward me."

She could do nothing for a moment but gape at him. As his words finally sank in, she seemed embarrassed, her face turning a deep shade of pink.

Yanking a hand through his hair, he apologized. "Forgive my impertinence, Christina. I should not have presumed that you would feel free to discuss so intimate a subject with me."

"Oh, no! Please don't apologize, Nicholas. I'm just taken aback that you would want to know about my feelings. I haven't been so obvious with my feelings, have I? Have I embarrassed you, as Helen has done with the duke? I was not aware I wore my emotions so—"

"Then you do!" he exclaimed, grinning broadly. "You do have feelings for me."

She looked down at Ty. "You must know I do."

He threw back his head and laughed. "That's marvelous!" he cried as he leaned over and kissed her on the cheek, surprising them both with his impulsiveness.

"Nicholas!" she gasped, but still wearing a hesitant smile.

"I need to see to my guests, but may we talk again tomorrow?"

She nodded, looking a little dazed.

He threw her another happy grin. "Tomorrow. Here in the garden."

With that, he got up and walked back into the house.

And the moment he closed the door, he realized he hadn't told her about his own feelings.

But no matter, he thought. He would see her tomorrow, and then everything in his life would be just the way he wanted it.

fourteen

"He asked you what?" Helen blurted out and quickly put a hand over her mouth when Christina hushed her for speaking too loudly.

Conflicting emotions had swirled in Christina's heart all night, allowing her only a few moments of sleep. Over and over she had gone through the conversation she and Nicholas shared. Over and over she tried to find a reasonable explanation for his asking her to reveal such personal feelings.

The only conclusion she could reach was he too had strong feelings for her.

Oh, if only he had voiced them!

So, unable to think objectively, she thought it wise to get Helen's opinion.

"He said he needed to know what my feelings were for him," she repeated, chewing her lip as she waited for Helen's reply.

"And you told him you cared very much for him," Helen surmised correctly.

"How did you know?"

Helen smiled. While it was true she wasn't good at dealing with her own love life, she was incredibly perceptive where others were concerned. "You are my oldest and dearest friend, Christina. How could I not see the love you have for him shining in your eyes when you thought no one was looking?"

Christina sighed, feeling tired and confused. "I tried so to fight my caring for him, Helen, truly I did. But the more he came out of his depressed state and opened up to us as a friend, the more I realized I was falling in love with him. But does his asking me about my feelings mean he has feelings for me too?"

Helen reached out and grasped her friend's hand. "Of course it does. I have believed for some time the earl cared for you. I am sure it is the reason why he has changed his mind about shutting himself off from the world."

Hope sprang up in her chest at hearing Helen's words, but something else worried her. "But my goal was to allow God to change him."

Helen gave Christina an exasperated look. "Have you not heard your father say over and over, God uses us to help Him do His work on earth? You were willing to face his bad manners and ill humor just because you believed God wanted you to help him. And you have, Christina! God has used you to help him!"

Christina smiled tentatively. "I suppose you're right. He has come to church and promises to attend every Sunday."

"Well, there you are!"

They were silent for a moment as they sat in the small garden of Christina's home. She allowed herself to begin to hope there might be a future for them. Perhaps what she thought was impossible might be possible after all.

With that in mind, Christina decided to go with Helen to Kenswick Hall and see how Mrs. Sanborne was coping with the new visitors at the estate.

They found her in the nursery folding Ty's diapers, but the nanny was not in her usual chipper mood. In fact, she was very upset.

"I'm awfully glad you ladies have come. Awfully, awfully glad," she told them, tears swimming in her downcast eyes.

"Whatever is the matter, Mrs. Sanborne?" Christina asked. "Has something happened?"

The older woman shook her head. "I'm awfully afraid that I shall be dismissed," she told them, her voice wobbly with worry. "I'm in an awfully dreadful state over this. You see, I overheard Lady Stanhope say that she wanted to bring someone she already knew into the home to be Ty's nanny, that she was awfully displeased with my work so far."

Christina patted her back. "But that is only her opinion, Mrs. Sanborne. It is not how Lord Thornton feels! He is awfully. . .I mean he is very pleased with how you have taken care of Ty. Never would he fire you!"

"The woman is a busybody!" Helen cried.

Christina, no matter how much she agreed, did not want to speak unkindly about someone behind their back. "Helen, I'm sure this can all be worked out. I will go and speak to Nicholas about it. I'm sure all will be well."

Mrs. Sanborne gave her an encouraged smile. "Oh, thank you, Dear. What would I do without you?"

"You would do fine, I'm sure." She dismissed her praise with a wave of her hand. "I'll be back directly."

Christina made her way to the stairs and down to the main hall of the house. She had not seen any of Nicholas's guests since she and Helen had entered, as they always did, through the servants' entrance.

She heard them, however, as she stepped off the bottom step. Their laughter drifted to her from the sitting room to her left. She paused, unsure if she should interrupt or not.

But then she thought of Nicholas and knew he would not mind if she went in to talk to him.

The door was already slightly ajar, so she pushed it enough so that she could slip inside.

For a moment, no one noticed her, so Christina had a chance to study the room. Nicholas caught her attention right away, sitting on the settee with a beautiful young woman with dark hair so artfully arranged it must have taken her maid hours to accomplish it. Her exquisite dress was stunning as well, the deep blue silk complimenting the creamy paleness of her skin.

Her first thought was that they looked so perfect sitting together. Nicholas grinned at something she was saying. Just the kind of woman an earl should marry—poised, self-assured, and a member of the *ton*.

She silently chastised herself for thinking so negatively and looked around to the others in the room.

Not surprisingly, Lady Stanhope was smiling charmingly at the distinguished couple sitting directly in front of her. Wealth and prestige emanated from the couple, so different were they from the simple ladies and gentlemen from Malbury.

And so different from Christina.

"Christina!" Nicholas called. She turned to see him stand and smile her way.

Relieved he was glad to see her, she stepped farther into the room, pretending not to see the familiar frown appearing on Lady Stanhope's face. "I'm sorry if I've intruded," she began hesitantly.

Perhaps, she thought, *I should not have been so bold!*

"Nonsense!" Nicholas assured her. "Please let me introduce

you to my guests. May I introduce Lord and Lady Delacourt? And this is their daughter, Lady Serena Delacourt." He then motioned toward Christina. "My lord and ladies, this is my neighbor and good friend, Miss Christina Wakelin."

Christina curtsied, smiling a greeting at the three of them. They barely nodded in return, eyeing her with a great deal of curious speculation.

Especially the younger Lady Delacourt.

Thanks to her father, Christina grew up confident in the person that she was. God was no respecter of persons, he'd often quoted. He loved everybody the same, no matter their class or how much money they had.

But now she did not feel so confident. She felt way out of her element, and all she wanted to do was run from Kenswick Hall and surround herself with people she knew and loved.

She was about to do just that when Nicholas asked, "You are here to remind me of my daily meeting, are you not?"

Taken off guard, Christina paused, then stammered, "Uh, meeting?" Then she realized he was trying to give them both an excuse to leave the room. "Oh! Yes. I thought. . .perhaps. . .I should come down and. . .uh. . .remind you. Of the meeting."

Christina refused to look at anyone but Nicholas, but she could feel their eyes on her and knew they were thinking the same thing she was—she had sounded like a complete idiot!

"I'm afraid I'll have to leave you to my aunt," he told everyone in the room. "I always meet with my nephew every day at this time, so I know you will understand if I hesitate to break our regular schedule."

"Nicholas!" his aunt spoke up. "Surely you can postpone for one day."

"Oh, no, please keep your schedule with your nephew,"

the elder Lady Delacourt chimed in. "Bonding with one's parent is so important at this age. I myself met with my daughter for one hour a day when she was a babe, and now we enjoy the closest of relationships."

Christina glanced at Serena Delacourt just in time to see the bored look she gave her mother at that comment. She didn't blame her. Christina couldn't imagine one hour a day being enough time for a parent to spend with their child.

"You are correct, Lady Delacourt," he responded with a nod.

After assuring them he would see them at dinner, Nicholas motioned for Christina to precede him out the door, which he shut firmly behind them.

"If you had shown up a minute later, I fear I might have gone mad!" he whispered, then grinned at her. "Listening to how many ladies were wearing pink at the last ball Lady Serena attended was not what I call stimulating conversation!"

"But she is quite beautiful, don't you think?" Christina said. "Very poised and I'm sure extremely accomplished."

"Accomplished in what, pray? Boring a man to tears?" He shook his head. "No, dear Christina. I know what you are saying and I'm telling you to put your mind at ease." They were walking out to the garden when Nicholas suddenly pulled her off the path and into a secluded nook.

He cupped her face with his large, strong hands and gazed at her as if she were the most important person in the world to him.

"Christina, I asked you yesterday what your feelings were concerning me, but in my excitement I neglected to tell you just what my feelings are for you."

Her heart felt as though it might pound right out of her chest. "And?" she prompted.

"My feelings are so great that I cannot envision a life without you," he stated fervently. "But I am afraid I am not worthy of you, Christina. You deserve so much better a man than I have been."

Christina's eyes filled with tears of wonderment and complete happiness. "It is the past, Nicholas. You are that man no more. You've allowed God to change you, you must realize that."

He caressed the sides of her face with his thumbs. "I know He is changing me. I've been studying the Scriptures and want the kind of relationship with God that you and your father have. I just feel as though I need to make restitution for some of my past misdeeds. That is why I have agreed to let my aunt invite half the *ton* to Kenswick Hall. When I ask your father for your hand, I want to be able to present to you a name of good standing—not one that has been sullied. Perhaps these visits will let me once again be in their favor."

"But, Nicholas, my father will see that you have changed. And, besides, you know I care nothing for London society. Why should I be bothered if they accept us or not?"

"But you must, Christina, for our sake, for Ty's sake, and for any other children we will have. We don't have to be in their inner circle, but it is always better to be on good terms with them."

Christina had to voice her most important concern. "But will not your marrying a commoner such as I ostracize you anyway?"

"The *ton* is a fickle and hypocritical lot! As charming and beautiful as you are, my dear, I daresay you would win over the most ardent critic," he assured her.

Christina was about to ask him how long they would

have to wait before he spoke to her father, but Mrs. Sanborne called her name from the other side of the garden. Sighing, she said, "As much as I hate it, I should probably let you go back to your guests." Then she remembered something. "Oh! Please reassure Mrs. Sanborne that you do not intend to let her go from her position. She overheard your aunt berating her competence as Ty's nanny."

Nicholas groaned. "She must have berated my new valet, Smith, in the same conversation, for he kept asking me this morning if his work was sufficient to my needs. I didn't understand why he was suddenly insecure when he'd been nothing less than swaggering before. Now, however, it all falls into place."

"I shall be glad when all your visits from London society are over with and your aunt has gone from Kenswick!" she confessed, unable to hide her frustration with the whole matter.

Nicholas laughed softly as he bent down to kiss her on the nose. "No more so than I," he agreed before kissing her again. This time on the lips.

"Now I shall go and say hello to my nephew before returning inside. I don't want to become a liar on top of everything else I have done," he teased as he left her standing alone.

Christina could not even remember telling him goodbye, so stunned was she at the warm touch from his lips. In fact, she might have stayed there all day had not Mrs. Sanborne called her name again, urging her to join them.

She and Nicholas exchanged a secret look when she approached. It was as if they both wanted to keep their news to themselves for awhile. After a moment, he went back inside and Christina stayed in the garden.

It took great effort to concentrate on the conversation as

the women chattered about the guests and wondered what styles they wore. Nicholas's lovely words kept swimming around her mind, thrilling her every time she recalled them. She wanted to remember them, dream of them for a few days, until Nicholas's promise came to fruition.

Until he asked her father for her hand.

fifteen

"I have paraded four exquisite young women in front of you in the last week and yet you show no inclination to make an offer to any of them!" Nicholas's aunt declared as she entered his suite of rooms unannounced. He was busy putting the finishing touches to one of his small figurines.

She stopped abruptly. "Whatever are you doing?"

Blowing away the remaining wood shavings, he set the figurine of his cat, licking one of its front paws, on the edge of his worktable.

Still somewhat bemused, Aunt Wilhelmina picked it up and studied the intricate detail. "You have the gift," she whispered with awe, her eyes still on the figurine.

He raised an eyebrow. "I beg your pardon?"

"My father, your grandfather, used to carve the most wonderful little statuettes and give them to the children of the village. I have five of them in my home in Stafford."

Stunned, Nicholas shook his head. "I don't remember him. I was only two or three when he died, and Father never mentioned it."

"Of course he wouldn't have. If memory serves me correctly, William used them as his targets when practicing his archery."

Nicholas chuckled. His father had been the consummate hunter and fisherman. He wouldn't have cared about a few chunks of decorative wood—not when they served his purpose better honing his own hobby!

"Now, back to your marriage," Aunt Wilhelmina began.

"What marriage?"

His aunt placed the carving back on his desk and folded her arms across her chest in a no-nonsense manner. "My point exactly. You must try to make a worthwhile effort if there is going to *be* a marriage! Really, Nicholas. You cannot shirk your responsibility to your nephew or your title. You must make a match, and the sooner the better."

Nicholas was so tired of playing his aunt's game. Because of the many guests she'd paraded in and out of his home, he had not spoken to Christina but a few minutes each day. And the day before, when he spoke to her, she'd said she would be too busy to come by for the next few days. She'd seemed preoccupied, even a little distant.

What in the world was she doing? Had she decided to move on with her life without him? Perhaps she'd decided to marry a farmer the vicar had picked out for her. . . .

"Nicholas, are you daydreaming?" his aunt scolded as she tapped on his table with her blue silk fan. "Will you stop dilly-dallying and start taking this seriously?"

"I already have," he stated firmly, deciding it was time to tell her of his true plans.

"I beg your pardon? What does this mean?"

"I have already chosen a bride."

When his aunt broke into a triumphant smile, Nicholas knew she had taken his words the wrong way. "Which one? The Delacourt girl? No! I know it's the beautiful blond one. . .Constance, I believe her name was."

"You misunderstand me, Aunt," he interrupted before she became too excited. "I intend to marry Christina Wakelin."

"That little vicar's daughter?" she cried with unbelief. For a moment, Nicholas was afraid she might faint from the shock, but she seemed to pull herself together. Taking a breath and clearing her throat, she told him, "Nicholas, Dear, girls such as that are for mild flirtations and amusement to a nobleman of your station. You do not, however, *marry* them."

"I'm in love with her," he stated bluntly.

She gave a trilling little laugh at those words. "Is that all? What has love to do with anything? Once you are married to a girl of good breeding, you'll soon forget about this lapse in judgment."

Nicholas grew irritated by her flippant attitude for all that he considered precious. He stood to his feet. "She is not a lapse, Aunt. She is the woman I intend to marry, the woman who will bear the next Earl of Kenswick."

Aunt Wilhelmina grabbed her fan and cooled her face in a rapid, erratic manner. "Do not say that, I beg you. You mustn't even joke about such a travesty!"

Nicholas replied calmly. "My mind is made up. There shall be no more discussion on this subject."

She did not speak for a moment, and Nicholas could not read her face. She made a show of smoothing the lace at her wrist. "And have you asked her father for her hand?" she said, a strange calmness to her voice.

Nicholas did not trust it. "No."

"Ah," she said and stood. "And what of the other guests I have invited? Would you have me cancel their invitations when some of them might already be on their way?"

Of course he could not do that. It would further cast a stain against his name to make such a social faux pas. "No, but issue no more invitations. At the week's end, I shall speak to Reverend Wakelin and make the announcement to the newspapers."

"Of course, Dear," she answered with a submissiveness that rang false in Nicholas's ears. "Just this week." He noticed she completely ignored his latter statement.

After she left, Nicholas did not dwell on his aunt's strange behavior. Instead, he stood and closed his eyes in a prayer to God.

"Let this week pass quickly, Lord," he prayed. "And prepare the vicar's heart so I might find favor with him at the week's end."

The latter request was the one thing Nicholas feared would foil his plans with Christina. The last time marriage was mentioned concerning his daughter, the vicar's feelings on the subject had been clear—he was not in favor of any connection between Christina and himself.

৯

Christina had worked tirelessly for two days as she helped Mrs. Ledbetter, a young mother in the village, care for her one-year-old twins as she delivered yet another baby. Her husband, a soldier, had recently left with his regiment for three months. The woman had no one to help her.

How fortunate for him, Christina thought in a rare moment of feeling sorry for herself. Although other women from the village had taken turns helping Christina, she had been there the entire time, with little sleep.

In the late afternoon, she was relieved by an older woman from the church who had reared eight children of her own. She told Christina to go home and rest.

Back at home, Christina was even too tired to eat. All

she wanted to do was fall into bed and sleep for the rest of the day and night.

Her father came out of his study as she reached the stairs and looked up from the book he'd been reading. He stepped forward to pat her on the head as if she were a little girl, then mumbled something about God rewarding her for her hard work. Since this was not unusual behavior, she smiled at him and started up the stairs.

She got no farther than the fourth step when a knock sounded at the door.

Mrs. Hopkins looked up at Christina as she hurried to answer it. "Were you expecting someone, Miss Christina?"

"No," she answered, wishing she could just ignore the knock. "I suppose you better answer it. I am not dressed to receive visitors, but with father deep in study, I suppose I'd better." She looked down at her soiled brown dress. "Perhaps it is someone in need."

But it wasn't, much to Christina's horror and dismay. There on the vicarage doorstep stood Lady Wilhelmina Stanhope, looking as out of place in the humble home as a fish in the desert. Draped in a mint green silk gown of the latest London fashion, she had the accessories to match, including a perfectly dyed umbrella she used as a cane.

"Lady Stanhope!" Christina greeted with a pleasantness she did not feel as she came back down the stairs. "To what do we owe this pleasure?"

Her ladyship's eyes widened as she perused Christina's dress. "I seem to have come at a bad time," she said. "I don't believe I've ever seen you look so dreadfully ill in all the time I've been at Kenswick."

It was all Christina could do to remain calm. What she

really wanted to do was demand that the horrible woman leave her home and take her critical words with her.

But, of course, she did not. If Nicholas could change his life, surely Lady Stanhope could also—with some time and a lot of effort.

"I've just come from the home of a young mother who has delivered a baby. I've been there for two days, helping her with her young twins," she explained, hoping the woman would take the hint that she was quite tired.

She did not. "I see," she said, although it was clear from her tone that she did not see and certainly did not understand. "I've come to have a word with you, Miss Wakelin. It is a matter of great importance."

Christina could not decline. "Why don't we go into the front parlor?" To her housekeeper, she asked, "Could you bring us some tea, Mrs. Hopkins?"

"I'll not be here that long," Lady Stanhope declared before the housekeeper could even nod her head.

Christina sighed and shook her head toward Mrs. Hopkins to let her know tea, apparently, would not be needed.

She led Lady Stanhope into the bright, cheerful room that was a favorite of Christina's with its yellow floral wallpaper and her mother's colorful paintings on the walls. She motioned for Lady Stanhope to take the sofa, and she did so, but not before casting a disapproving glance around the room.

"Your living arrangements are very small, Miss Wakelin," she observed, keeping a hand on the handle of her upright umbrella. "Have you but one servant?"

"No, we also have a cook," Christina replied a little defensively. "My father and I have always found our home quite sufficient for our needs."

"Ah. And your mother?"

"She died when I was a small child. Lady Stanhope, did you not say you had a matter of great importance to discuss with me?"

The woman's back stiffened at Christina's blunt remark. "Let me get right to the point. I know you have been a great assistance to my nephew these last few months and helped him to overcome the troubled state that prevailed upon him after he left the war."

"Well, I was simply doing what I felt God led me to do," Christina replied. "I knew he could overcome his bitterness and pain once he—"

"Yes, yes, Dear. There's no need to go on about it," Lady Stanhope interrupted. "The point I am trying to make is that because he was weak, and I might say *vulnerable*, during this time, he has allowed his emotions, it seems, to replace his good judgment." She leaned forward, giving Christina a hard look. "You understand what I am saying, don't you?"

"Nicholas told you about his feelings toward me," Christina whispered in wonderment.

Lady Stanhope gripped her umbrella, tapping it on the floor for emphasis. "He says he intends to marry you!"

Christina smiled widely.

"Do not look so happy about it, young lady. I'll have you know that by marrying you he is jeopardizing his entire future and bringing shame upon a family title that has flourished for six generations!"

Christina tried valiantly to hold her temper. "How? How am I jeopardizing his future and bringing shame to him?"

The elder woman tapped hard on the floor again. "Who is your family? What are their connections other than some minor baronet in your family tree? What do you bring to this marriage if not position? A large dowry perhaps?" she said snidely, peering down her nose at Christina.

"I bring him love and happiness!"

"Humpft!" the woman sniffed.

Christina stood with hands on hips. "I also bring to him a relationship that is grounded in God's love, stable and unwavering."

Lady Stanhope stood as well. "What good is love if all of society snubs him and his offspring? How happy will you be watching his peers laugh behind his back or, worse, feel sorry that at a moment of weakness he allowed himself to settle so far beneath him! How stable will your marriage be when he wakes up one morning realizing he made the worst mistake of his life by marrying a vicar's daughter?"

Tears prickled behind Christina's eyes as the woman's words drove like daggers into her heart. "Is that what you think?" she asked hoarsely. "Do you believe he only thinks he loves me because he is grateful for my help?"

"Think about it, Dear," she soothed. "Nicholas was once the most sought after nobleman in England. He knew of you even then, did he not?"

Christina nodded slowly, not wanting to hear any more.

"Had he ever sought you out before?"

"No, but I was young when he left."

Lady Stanhope smiled. "But let us be honest with ourselves, shall we? If nothing had happened to Nicholas, do you think he still would have chosen you for his bride?"

Christina's mind flew back to Nicholas as a young man and how annoyed he always seemed to be with her. She replayed the scene at the tree and his reaction to finding out who she was.

He had been appalled at the revelation!

Perhaps Lady Stanhope was right. Perhaps he cared for her out of a sense of gratefulness or, worse, because she had practically thrown herself into his life, giving him no choice but to think he needed her around him permanently.

Weary from the last two days and now with the realization that she was about to lose her true love, Christina sat back down on her chair, clasping her hands tightly in her lap. "I do not want him to ever feel shame or regret for marrying me," she stated, her tone listless.

"Of course you don't, Dear," the woman mollified, taking the seat next to her. "I have a lovely estate in Stafford. Why don't you use my carriage to go there for a fortnight? It will allow you an occasion to sort through your feelings and permit your heart to heal." She reached out to pat Christina's hand. "It will also give Nicholas a chance to sort through his emotions. With you being there, perhaps he'll be able to see his way more clearly and make decisions that are right, not only for him, but for his family as well."

Christina didn't want to go to Stafford or anywhere else. All she wanted to do was run up to her room and cry her heart out.

But neither did she want Nicholas to regret marrying her. Only with her gone would he be able to understand what was best for him.

"I will go," she said at last.

"Excellent!" Lady Stanhope exclaimed as she used her umbrella to stand. "No, please do not stand. I will show myself out. If you'll have your things packed and ready by morning, my driver will be by with the carriage."

Christina did not remember saying good-bye. All she could do was cover her face as her tears finally came forth. "Why, dear God? Why do I have to let him go, when it was You who seemed to bring us together? How could I have been so wrong?"

But she had known all along that a match between them was impossible. She had told herself, even warned herself, it could not be—but allowed hope to flourish anyway.

Now she loved him.

And now she must let him go.

sixteen

"I think it's quite noble how you spend time with your nephew, my lord," Lady Judith Grisham told Nicholas with what he considered an excessively high and irritating tone as they strolled in his garden. Ty was sound asleep on his shoulder, since he'd learned that having the baby with him stopped any ideas of romance from whatever lady was visiting him.

"I believe that time spent with your child can only improve their chances of growing up to be an adult of extreme confidence and abilities," he told her, trying not to wince over having sounded so stuffy.

"Uh, yes, I suppose so. But do you think that some time apart from him would benefit the child as well?" she asked hopefully.

"No."

"Oh." Nicholas heard her sigh as they completed their lap around the garden.

The Grishams were the last guests, and he was grateful for that. They'd be leaving today, and that meant he could finally get on with his life.

If she were still willing to marry him, that is. Nicholas had not seen Christina in five days, and he was beginning to worry. Every time he questioned Helen about it, she would only tell him Christina had been very busy and could not come. It was clear she didn't want to talk about it.

To make matters worse, thanks to his aunt, he'd had no

time to ride out to the vicarage himself.

And he was becoming worried.

Ty chose that moment to wake up and cry, giving Nicholas an excuse to leave Lady Grisham's company. "I do beg your pardon, but I believe he must be ready for his nap."

"Must you be the one to take him to the nursery?" she asked, allowing her exasperation to show.

"I fear I must." He started to walk away from her toward the side entrance.

"But. . .but will I see you again before my family departs?" she called out.

"Certainly."

She began to look hopeful again, a smile blooming on her attractive face.

"I shall meet you in the front hall to say my good-byes before you embark on your journey home."

She stopped smiling.

As Nicholas bolted up the stairs, he felt a sense of relief. All the tedious entertaining was almost at an end, and now he could get back to his life and to Christina.

But first he must go and speak with her father.

Three hours later, Nicholas rode on horseback to the vicarage. Excitement mixed with nervousness coursed through his veins as he thought about speaking to her father.

He couldn't wait until Christina was his wife. The time spent apart from her these last days only confirmed to him that he could not live without her.

She was everything he could ever imagine in a mate. She'd even seen him at his worst and did not give up on him.

Though he'd committed a social faux pas by ending his engagement to his former fiancée, he could only thank God he'd done it now. He could not imagine spending his life with any woman other than the redheaded, outspoken girl who had climbed his tree and fallen right into his arms and life, changing him forever.

He tied his horse to a post in front of the house and made his way to the door. He did not understand the frightened look that came upon the housekeeper's face when she saw who it was at the door.

"My. . .my lord!" she stammered. "What can I do for you?"

Nicholas smiled at her. Perhaps it was his title that made her so nervous. "You could call your mistress for starters. I would very much like to speak with her."

Her eyes darted to a space behind the door and then back to him. "I'm afraid you can't."

He blinked. "I beg your pardon? Is she ill?"

"No, it's just that she is not here, my lord."

"Oh, I see," Nicholas replied. He'd not seen Helen today, so perhaps Christina was visiting her. "Well, could I possibly speak to the vicar then?"

The woman seemed relieved he'd dropped the questions about Christina. She stepped back and motioned for him to go to a side parlor. "Wait here, my lord, and I will get him for you."

Nicholas nodded and went into the room. As he waited, he admired the paintings that hung on all four walls.

"Those were my wife's paintings." Nicholas spun around to find the vicar standing in the doorway. The man nodded toward the painting Nicholas had been studying. "She painted that one when she found out she was pregnant with Christina." It was a portrait of a young woman sitting in a meadow cradling a baby in her arms.

"They are all quite amazing," Nicholas complimented honestly.

"She was quite an amazing woman. Not a day passes that I don't miss her." His thoughts seemed to drift to the past as he gazed at the portrait. Finally, he looked back at Nicholas. "I'm sorry, I've drifted off a bit. Mrs. Hopkins said you wanted to see me?"

"Yes, Sir. I was hoping to speak to Christina before I had this talk with you, but she seems to be out and about this afternoon," he began. The vicar interrupted with a concerned frown.

"I'm sorry, but I thought you knew," Reverend Wakelin said.

"Knew what, Sir?"

"Christina has left Malbury for a brief holiday at your aunt's estate in Stafford. I thought perhaps your aunt or even my daughter would have mentioned it."

Nicholas reached out to grip the back of a chair nearby. "No one told me. When I asked Helen about her, she told me only that Miss Wakelin was very busy."

The vicar studied Nicholas for a moment, his keen eyes missing nothing. "Perhaps we should sit down."

"No! I must know, Sir, how this trip came about. When did my aunt speak to her?"

Reverend Wakelin scratched his head as he thought about it. "I suppose it was three days ago. I did not see her, but Christina told me about the visit and about your aunt's invitation." He shook his head, his face showing his concern. "I did not like the look of her, my lord. She'd been up for nearly forty-eight hours helping one of our young mothers who'd delivered a child. I could not deny her the trip when she seemed so determined to leave."

Confused and a little hurt by this news, Nicholas began to pace about the small room. "She mentioned nothing else about the conversation with my aunt? Did she seem upset or angry?"

"No to both questions, my lord." After a hesitant pause, he said, "You mentioned before that you came to speak with me. To what does it pertain?"

Nicholas stopped and looked directly at the vicar. "I came to ask for your daughter's hand in marriage," he told him bluntly. "I spoke to Christina a week ago and told her how I felt, but I have not seen her since."

The vicar did not seem very surprised. "I see," he said. "And does she return your feelings, my lord?"

"Yes!" he declared. "She knew I would be coming to speak to you after my guests left. I thought it was understood she would be waiting for me."

"Do you love her?"

"With all my heart, Sir," Nicholas answered with great feeling as the two men shared an understanding look. "I must go and see her!"

Nicholas started to leave when the vicar stopped him. "One moment, my lord. I believe I have more to speak to you about before you go to her."

Nicholas bit back his irritation at being delayed, reminding himself he needed this man's approval if Christina was to be his wife. But it was late in the day and traveling would not be easy. "Yes, of course," he relented and sat in the chair the vicar motioned him toward.

Sitting across from him, the vicar began, "Christina tells me you have changed a great deal from when she first met you again on your estate." Nicholas nodded. "The fact you are titled and considered a good catch by all of society, despite your past reputation, does not matter to me in the least. What I am most concerned about is your spiritual condition. Are you a follower of Christ, my lord?"

Nicholas answered sincerely. "Yes, Sir. At times I have blamed God for my circumstances, but not anymore. Christina has shown me what it means to be a Christian, what it means to put my faith in the One who created me."

"Have you changed your mind only because of Christina?"

"No. I've started to believe in God again because I needed Him in my life, Sir."

"Then you indeed have my blessing," the vicar replied with a smile, his gaze going to the clock on the mantle. "But if you want to reach Stafford before midnight, I would say you should be on your way."

Nicholas stood up and shook his future father-in-law's hand enthusiastically. "That is just what I intend, Sir, and thank you. You shall not regret giving your blessing!"

"Please see that I don't!" the vicar said with a teasing light in his eyes.

Nicholas wasted no time in riding back to Kenswick and ordering one of the stable boys to ready his horse for the long journey.

"You're not going to take the carriage, Sir?" the young man asked, aghast.

"No, it will be quicker on horseback. I'll just need to go inside the house for a few things. See that the horse is ready."

It didn't take long for Nicholas to get what money he might need and the betrothal ring that had belonged to his family for six generations. He retrieved both from the safe in his study. It was there he encountered his aunt.

"What are you doing?" she demanded from the doorway.

"I am going to undo whatever damage you have wrought concerning Christina," he answered coldly.

She grabbed his arm as he passed, looking down at the tiny box in his hand. "What are you intending to do with that?"

He jerked his arm free. "Just what you think I am going to do with it, Aunt. I don't know what lies you told her, but I intend to convince her to be my bride. When I return, I will expect you to be gone!"

"How dare you speak to me in that manner!"

He stepped close to her, staring her straight in the eyes. "And how dare you try to interfere with my life. You had no right to speak to her."

His aunt took a wary step back. "I only told her the truth, Nicholas. Marrying the girl will only bring more shame to your name and title. The *ton* will never accept her!"

"I don't care what the *ton* thinks!" he growled.

"You will regret this! Mark my words!"

"I will regret it if I don't leave right now and bring her back!" With that he left the room, stopping to speak with Pierce before he got to the front door.

"Inform Mrs. Sanborne I will be gone for tonight, but I will return by tomorrow."

Pierce's face wore a proud smile. "I will, my lord. And might I say Miss Christina will be a welcome addition to this household."

Nicholas shook his head with a chuckle. "One of these days, Pierce, your eavesdropping will get you into trouble."

"You are probably right, my lord." He opened the door with a bow. "Bring her home safely."

❧

Hartshorne Castle was a truly amazing place. Having been

refurbished over the centuries, the castle was surprisingly lavish and comfortable. But for Christina, it was hard to enjoy any of the beauty or history about the place. For three long days she'd walked up to the tower near her bedroom and sat staring out over the vast countryside. She'd cried, felt sorry for herself at times, but mainly wondered how Nicholas was doing and if he missed her as much as she missed him.

She even imagined he might come and get her, but as the days passed, it became unlikely he would do so. If he loved her, surely he would have come the day she left.

"Can I fix you a spot of tea, Ma'am?" one of the young maids asked from the open door. Christina saw that she was staring at her with worry, much like all the other staff had done since she'd arrived. She'd tried to pretend everything was all right but had been unable to carry off the charade.

"No, thank you," Christina answered. "I'm just going to sit here for a few moments before I turn in."

"Yes, Ma'am," the maid replied, but as she went back down the stairs, Christina heard her murmur, "Poor dear."

Sighing, Christina looked back out into the dark night from her seat by the window. There was no moon out, but the stars were shining brightly, twinkling like tiny jewels all around her.

She closed her eyes, letting the cool night breeze blow over her features, and she prayed like she had so often in the past few days. She prayed that God would allow her pain to cease, that He would help her to move on with her life.

A life without the Earl of Kenswick.

Weary, she folded her arms on the window seat and lay her head on them.

And dreamed of Nicholas.

seventeen

Nicholas tried not to think of the pain shooting through his wounded leg as he climbed the tower steps of Hartshorne Castle. Riding a horse was probably not the smartest thing for his health, but he knew the pain would be worth it all once he got to Christina.

When he reached the top of the stairs, he found her right where the young servant said she'd be.

His heart had broken when she told him how unhappy Christina had been—how the servants had heard her cry when she thought no one was around.

What had his aunt done to the woman who had been so full of life and joy? Could the thought of losing him have brought so much pain?

If so, he knew she truly did love him, just as much as he loved her.

Gently he reached out to tuck an errant curl behind her ear, then allowed himself to caress her pale cheek. Her eyes fluttered, but still she did not awaken.

"Christina," he said softly as he knelt down beside her. "Wake up, my love. Wake up so I might talk with you."

She slowly opened her eyes. "Nicholas?" she murmured groggily as she lifted her head and tried to focus. "Nicholas!" she cried aloud once she realized it was really he.

She held out her hands to him and he took them, kissing

each one. "My love, are you really so surprised to see me?" he chided with a smile. "Surely you knew I would come."

Christina shook her head, and Nicholas could tell that the fog of sleep was clearing. "But it's been three days. I thought. . ."

"I just found out this afternoon. Helen had been telling me only that you were busy. I didn't know anything about you leaving Malbury."

"I felt I had to leave. After your aunt's visit, I—"

"Yes, my aunt," he said, letting his frustration show. "What exactly did she say that caused you to leave?"

Christina stood and walked to the other side of the room. "She told me the truth, Nicholas."

He stood also, but stayed where he was. "And what truth was that?"

"That what you feel toward me is only gratitude. I came into your life when you were vulnerable and helped you get through it. In time you'll come to regret your decision to marry me, perhaps even feel embarrassed you married so far beneath you."

"Do you really think me so shallow or perhaps so unconnected with my feelings that I would confuse love with gratitude?" he roared, throwing his hands up to emphasize his words. "What about your feelings? Are they so weak that the first person who comes and tries to destroy what we have is actually successful?"

She gasped. "That is quite unfair! I left because I wanted to do what was best for you. If being married to me was going to cause your peers to snub you or, worse, to feel sorry for you, then I was going to spare you that."

Shaking his head, he stared at her for a long moment, reading the sincerity and love in her eyes. Slowly, he began to walk toward her. "What's best for me is you, Christina. You must know that."

She blinked as if she were trying not to cry. "You must be sure, Nicholas. I could not bear to see you unhappy. I would. . ."

"Shhh!" He pulled her into his arms and kissed her on the lips. After a moment, he leaned back and smiled lovingly into her shining eyes. "I love you, Christina, and that love will never go away, no matter who disapproves of us. Will you marry me and take away this misery I've been feeling for the last five days without you?"

"Oh, Nicholas. That was so beautifully spoken, I think I might cry," she said, sniffing.

"Do you think perhaps you could answer my question before you cry? I do feel a bit at loose ends here!"

She laughed as she threw her arms around his neck. "I love you with all my heart, Nicholas. Of course I'll marry you!"

He hugged her to him and closed his eyes, soaking in how wonderful it felt to hold her in his arms.

"I have something for you." He stepped back and reached in his coat pocket for the small velvet box. When he opened it, her eyes grew round at the size of the ruby within. The stone was centered in an ornate setting of gold, surrounded by small diamonds.

"Nicholas," she whispered as he took the ring and reached for her hand, placing it on her finger.

"There! It fits you perfectly. Just as you fit me perfectly," he whispered back. "God brought you to me, Christina, and I'll thank Him every day of my life."

She smiled, turning her hand so that she could lace her fingers with his. "I knew He led me to you. I just didn't realize the full purpose. Actually, I couldn't imagine an earl ever being interested in an ordinary vicar's daughter."

"Ah, but there is nothing ordinary about you, my love. Ordinary girls do not climb trees to save cats or nurse half the animals in the shire back to health. Nor do they hide puppies in ballrooms or badger a bad-tempered man into realizing that life is too precious to waste feeling sorry for oneself."

Christina winced. "Could we just forget about the tree incident? I'm not really proud of that particular escapade."

Nicholas laughed. "Oh, no. It shall be a tale that will be told to our children and to their children. Not everyone can say their true love fell from above and directly into their arms."

She suddenly remembered something. "Oh no! What about my father? Suppose he does not give us his blessing? He's always been a little wary where you are concerned."

Nicholas put a finger to her lips and smiled reassuringly. "I've already asked him. That's how I found out about you being gone from Malbury. Though he didn't know the details, he explained about my aunt's visit and where you had gone afterward."

"And his answer was. . .?"

"His answer was yes. But only after he was sure I was the kind of man you needed—the Christian man I needed to become."

He cradled her face with both hands. "In a very short time, Christina, you are going to be the Countess of Kenswick. Do you suppose you could get used to all the bowing and scraping that goes with the title?"

"Oh my," she cried after a quick intake of breath. "I have no idea what is required of a countess." She looked worried for a moment. "I do not have to give up all my animals, do I?"

Nicholas laughed as he leaned down and gave her another kiss. "You may have as many animals as you please as long as you keep them out of the ballroom."

She smiled. "I think I can manage that!"

❧

Two months later, Reverend Wakelin married Christina and Nicholas in the parish church. After the ceremony, Christina stood with her husband on the lawn of Kenswick Hall as their guests mingled about.

She sighed happily as she felt Nicholas's hand on her back, drawing her close to him. "Happy?" he asked.

"Very." And she was. So very happy that, at last, he was her husband.

What made this occasion even more joyous was the support he'd received from high-ranking members of the *ton*. She'd met so many noble families in the last two months, and though they were hesitant at first, they all seemed to accept her into their elite group.

Christina was glad, not because being a part of them was important to her, but because she knew it was important to Nicholas to restore his family's good name.

"Did you see Ty when Mrs. Sanborne brought him down earlier? Fine-looking little man, don't you think?"

"Just like his handsome uncle," she acknowledged as someone walking from the courtyard into the side lawn caught her attention. The man looked so much like Nicholas, Christina thought he might be a cousin.

"Nicholas, who is that man over there?"

Nicholas looked to where Christina pointed, and she felt

him tense as if shocked at what he saw. "I cannot believe my eyes," he whispered hoarsely, shaking his head. "This cannot be. . . ."

"Who is it, Nicholas? Why does this man upset you?"

"It's my brother!" he gasped.

"What?"

"My brother. Christina, that is my brother, alive and breathing, walking across my lawn!"

☙

Watching his brother stride toward them was the most surreal occurrence Nicholas had ever experienced. As if in a trance, he walked out to meet him.

Thomas Thornton saw him also, and with a smile Nicholas new so well, he waved at him.

The two men embraced before speaking a word, slapping each other heartily on the back. Finally, Nicholas drew back, holding his brother by the shoulders as he studied him.

"You look quite healthy for a dead man," he said, his voice quavering with emotion.

Thomas chuckled. "I'm not dead yet, Brother. Almost, but God saw fit to save me."

Nicholas's eyes moved over his brother once again. "What happened, Thom? Why were you reported dead?"

Thom shook his head. "Our ship capsized in a bad storm, and a small group of sailors and I were able to cut loose one of the life boats and hold on until the storm passed. We were rescued by a merchant ship two days later, but, unfortunately, they were sailing to Canada to drop off a load of goods, so it took awhile to get back and notify my superiors in the Royal Navy that I had survived." He spread his arms out to indicate his lack of uniform. "And as you can see, I've also resigned my commission. I've had quite enough of the sea."

"How long have you been back?" Nicholas asked with a frown.

"About a fortnight. You see, after speaking to the navy, I went straight to Rosehaven to see. . .Anne." Thom's voice broke.

"Then you know."

He nodded. "I hate that I was not there for her, Nicholas. Even though our marriage was arranged by our fathers, I was truly fond of her. I might have grown to love her if given the proper time."

"Well, you must also be aware you are the father of a very bright and handsome little boy!"

"Indeed, I am! Can you take me to him?" he asked eagerly.

"Of course."

"Nicholas!" Christina called as he turned to see her walking toward him. She'd obviously given him time to speak to his brother, but curiosity had gotten the better of her. He smiled as he noticed her eyes darting back and forth between his brother and himself.

"Isn't this the vicar's daughter?" Thomas asked. "The mischievous scamp who used to play tricks on you as a child?"

Nicholas chuckled. "It is indeed." Smiling teasingly, he put an arm around Christina as she came up beside him. "Thomas, meet my wife. I believe you two already know each other."

Thomas's eyes widened as he stared at them. "But I thought you. . .uh. . ." He let his voice drift, unsure of how to say what he wanted to say.

"Were to marry someone else? Yes, I was, but it's a long story for another day. Suffice it to say God sent this special woman into my life again, and I knew I would be a fool to let her get away."

"It's so wonderful to see you are alive, Lord Thornton. This is truly the best wedding present we could have asked for," Christina told him.

Still dazed at the news, Thomas shook his head as he smiled at her. "Little Christina, the vicar's daughter," he mused. "I have kept many a sailor entertained on long journeys across the ocean with tales of your antics as a child."

"Not you too!" she groaned as Nicholas laughed.

"Wait until you hear what she's done lately!" he trumpeted, ignoring the small fist pounding him on the arm at the suggestion.

"I can't wait!" Thomas replied eagerly. "But before you ruin your wedding day, why don't we go and see my son."

Once they had gone back to the house, both Christina and Nicholas watched from the nursery doorway as Thomas reverently picked up his small son and held him close to his chest. A tear ran down his cheek as he bent to kiss the whisper-fine hair on his soft head.

"I know this means Ty will no longer be ours to raise, but I cannot be too disappointed when I see how much Thomas loves him," Christina whispered to her new husband. "I shall miss him, but I know he will be well taken care of."

Nicholas bent and placed a kiss on her hair. "Rosehaven is not very far from here. We'll see them often. And once our children are born, perhaps it will make the pain of losing Ty easier to bear."

She sighed. "Our children. I like the sound of that."

"I suppose one consolation will be that he'll have to take Mrs. Sanborne with him."

Christina put her hand over her mouth to hide her smile. "But I was planning on hiring her back once our first child was born!" she teased.

"Then I shall begin now to search the countryside for a replacement, just to ensure you don't!"

She laughed softly, turning her face upward to look at him. "Even though you can be a bit boorish at times, I love you very much, Lord Thornton." Her tone matched her mischievous grin.

"Although you nearly broke my back falling on me from out of that tree, and you want to turn my home into a menagerie, I love you very much too, Lady Thornton."

Nicholas nodded toward his brother. "I hope he finds the same happiness in life I have. He truly deserves it after all he's been through."

"Do you think he'll ever remarry?"

"I hope so," he answered softly. "Perhaps a young lady will fall out of *his* tree."

"It would take a miracle!" she declared, shaking her head.

Nicholas looked down at her with love in his eyes. "It just so happens I believe in them."

A Letter To Our Readers

Dear Reader:

In order that we might better contribute to your reading enjoyment, we would appreciate your taking a few minutes to respond to the following questions. We welcome your comments and read each form and letter we receive. When completed, please return to the following:

Fiction Editor
Heartsong Presents
PO Box 719
Uhrichsville, Ohio 44683

1. Did you enjoy reading *The Vicar's Daughter* by Kimberley Comeaux?
   ❏ Very much! I would like to see more books by this author!
   ❏ Moderately. I would have enjoyed it more if

   _____

   _____

   _____

2. Are you a member of **Heartsong Presents**? ❏ Yes ❏ No
   If no, where did you purchase this book? _____

   _____

3. How would you rate, on a scale from 1 (poor) to 5 (superior), the cover design? _____

4. On a scale from 1 (poor) to 10 (superior), please rate the following elements.

   ____ Heroine   ____ Plot
   ____ Hero   ____ Inspirational theme
   ____ Setting   ____ Secondary characters

5. These characters were special because?_____

_____

_____

6. How has this book inspired your life?_____

_____

_____

7. What settings would you like to see covered in future
   Heartsong Presents books? _____

_____

_____

8. What are some inspirational themes you would like to see
   treated in future books? _____

_____

_____

9. Would you be interested in reading other **Heartsong
   Presents** titles? ❑ Yes   ❑ No

10. Please check your age range:
    ❑ Under 18   ❑ 18-24
    ❑ 25-34   ❑ 35-45
    ❑ 46-55   ❑ Over 55

Name_____

Occupation _____

Address _____

City_____ State_____ Zip_____

TUCSON

Travel back in time to the 1870s when a small fort protected settlers of the Arizona desert—and a small town called Tucson was beginning to flourish. Meet the women who made faith, hope, and love blossom under the blazing sun.

Follow the fascinating life journeys of four pioneering women. Can they learn to love the land, its Creator, and the men who tame the wild desert?

Historical, paperback, 480 pages, 5 ³/₁₆" x 8"

❤ ❤ ❤ ❤ ❤ ❤ ❤ ❤ ❤ ❤ ❤ ❤ ❤ ❤ ❤ ❤

❤ ❤ ❤ ❤ ❤ ❤ ❤ ❤ ❤ ❤ ❤ ❤ ❤ ❤ ❤ ❤

Heartsong ♥

------- Presents -------

Great Inspirational Romance at a Great Price!

Heartsong Presents books are inspirational romances in contemporary and historical settings, designed to give you an enjoyable, spirit-lifting reading experience. You can choose wonderfully written titles from some of today's best authors like Peggy Darty, Sally Laity, Tracie Peterson, Colleen L. Reece, Debra White Smith, and many others.

When ordering quantities less than twelve, above titles are $3.25 each.
Not all titles may be available at time of order.

BLT

*H*EARTSONG ♥ PRESENTS

Love Stories Are Rated G!

That's for godly, gratifying, and of course, great! If you love a thrilling love story but don't appreciate the sordidness of some popular paperback romances, **Heartsong Presents** is for you. In fact, **Heartsong Presents** is the premiere inspirational romance book club featuring love stories where Christian faith is the primary ingredient in a marriage relationship.

Sign up today to receive your first set of four, never-before-published Christian romances. Send no money now; you will receive a bill with the first shipment. You may cancel at any time without obligation, and if you aren't completely satisfied with any selection, you may return the books for an immediate refund!

Imagine. . .four new romances every four weeks—two historical, two contemporary—with men and women like you who long to meet the one God has chosen as the love of their lives. . .all for the low price of $10.99 postpaid.

To join, simply complete the coupon below and mail to the address provided. **Heartsong Presents** romances are rated G for another reason: They'll arrive Godspeed!

YES! Sign me up for Hearts♥ng!

NEW MEMBERSHIPS WILL BE SHIPPED IMMEDIATELY!
Send no money now. We'll bill you only $10.99 postpaid with your first shipment of four books. Or for faster action, call toll free 1-800-847-8270.

NAME ———————————————————————

ADDRESS ——————————————————————

CITY————————————STATE ———— ZIP————

MAIL TO: HEARTSONG PRESENTS, P.O. Box 721, Uhrichsville, Ohio 44683
or visit www.heartsongpresents.com